"Meggie. You didn't g[...] yourself, now, did you[...] softly accused.

Megan's throat clamped tight. Her face flaming, she couldn't speak.

Nate Bravo was her most precious, hopeless fantasy. And he was here with her tonight. Because she had begged him to help her make a baby. And, in the end, he had been unable to refuse her need.

In twenty years Nate had never made any promises to her. He had always been honest. Brutally so. So Megan had thought she would never lie down with him. Because she wanted forever. And Nate wanted to be free.

Yet here they were. On their wedding night. One moment in time that would never last and never come again.

"Meggie?" Nate prompted.

As she stared at her new husband's sculpted chest, she attempted a quavering smile.

"Hell, Meggie..." Nate whispered.

Dear Reader,

Spring is in the air! It's the perfect time to pick wildflowers, frolic outdoors…and fall in love. And this March, Special Edition has an array of love stories that set the stage for romance!

Bestselling author Victoria Pade delivers an extra-special THAT SPECIAL WOMAN! title. The latest installment in her popular A RANCHING FAMILY series, *Cowboy's Love* is about a heroine who passionately reunites with the rugged rancher she left behind. Don't miss this warm and wonderful tale about love lost—and found again.

Romantic adventure is back in full force this month when the MONTANA MAVERICKS: RETURN TO WHITEHORN series continues with *Wife Most Wanted* by Joan Elliott Pickart—a spirited saga about a wanted woman who unwittingly falls for the town's sexiest lawman! And don't miss *Marriage by Necessity,* the second book in Christine Rimmer's engaging CONVENIENTLY YOURS miniseries.

Helen R. Myers brings us *Beloved Mercenary,* a poignant story about a gruff, brooding hero who finds new purpose when a precious little girl—and her beautiful mother—transform his life. And a jaded businessman gets much more than he bargained for when he conveniently marries his devoted assistant in *Texan's Bride* by Gail Link. Finally this month, to set an example for his shy teenage son, a confirmed loner enters into a "safe" relationship with a pretty stranger in *The Rancher Meets His Match* by Patricia McLinn.

I hope you enjoy this book, and each and every story to come!

Sincerely,

Tara Gavin
Senior Editor and Editorial Coordinator

Please address questions and book requests to:
Silhouette Reader Service
U.S.: 3010 Walden Ave., P.O. Box 1325, Buffalo, NY 14269
Canadian: P.O. Box 609, Fort Erie, Ont. L2A 5X3

CHRISTINE RIMMER

MARRIAGE BY NECESSITY

Silhouette®

SPECIAL ▼ EDITION®

Published by Silhouette Books

America's Publisher of Contemporary Romance

For Susan Crosby,
the best kind of friend,
one who inspires, instructs
and makes me laugh.

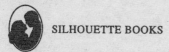 SILHOUETTE BOOKS

ISBN 0-373-24161-5

MARRIAGE BY NECESSITY

Copyright © 1998 by Christine Rimmer

Printed in U.S.A.

CHRISTINE RIMMER

came to her profession the long way around. Before settling down to write about the magic of romance, she'd been an actress, a sales clerk, a janitor, a model, a phone sales representative, a teacher, a waitress, a playwright and an office manager. Now that she's finally found work that suits her perfectly, she insists she never had a problem keeping a job—she was merely gaining "life experience" for her future as a novelist. Those who know her best withhold comment when she makes such claims; they are grateful that she's at last found steady work. Christine is grateful, too—not only for the joy she finds in writing, but for what waits when the day's work is through: a man she loves who loves her right back and the privilege of watching their children grow and change day to day. She lives with her family in Oklahoma.

THE BRAVOS

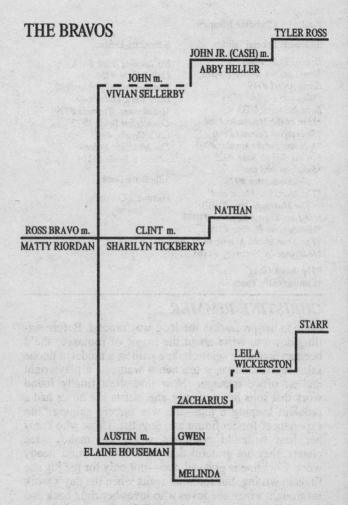

TYLER ROSS

JOHN JR. (CASH) m.
ABBY HELLER

JOHN m.
VIVIAN SELLERBY

NATHAN

ROSS BRAVO m.   CLINT m.
MATTY RIORDAN   SHARILYN TICKBERRY

STARR

LEILA
WICKERSTON

ZACHARIUS

AUSTIN m.   GWEN
ELAINE HOUSEMAN

MELINDA

(Broken lines indicate previous marriages)

Chapter One

In the pool area of the Hollywood Paradise Hotel, palm fronds swayed softly in a balmy summer breeze—a breeze only minimally tainted with smog. Tourists laughed and splashed in the pool. Gorgeous men and women lay on chaise lounges, dressed in skimpy swimwear and soaking up rays. Not far from the pool, at the Tropicana Poolside Bar, men in business suits enjoyed the shade and took their whiskey or vodka over ice. Meanwhile, at a table closer to the pool, a group of gray-haired ladies in bright-colored caftans drank strawberry daiquiris and argued over whether or not they had time to visit Universal Studios that day.

Four floors above the fun, a glass door stood open on a small balcony. In the room beyond the door, Megan May Kane lay on the bed and stared up at the ceiling fan that turned slowly overhead. Megan sighed. She hardly heard the happy laughter from below. Her lips moved. She was praying silently for the phone to ring.

When it did, she sat straight up and cried out, "Oh!"

It rang again. Megan put a hand to her heart and made herself take three deep, slow breaths. She told herself that she would be calm. Still, her hand shook when she reached for the receiver.

"H-hello?"

"Meggie?" The deep voice came out of her past, out of her dreams, out of her future as she had once dared to imagine it might be.

Her foolish heart soared. He had found her message on that machine of his. And he had actually called back.

"Meggie, are you there?"

"Uh, yes." She gulped, paused, breathed slowly. In. And then out. "Yes, Nate. I'm here."

"What the hell are you doing in L.A.?"

"I'm…" How to explain this, how to even *begin?* A hot jolt of anger pulsed through her—fury at her dead father.

"Meggie, are you all right?"

She steeled herself, ordered the pointless rage away. "Yes. I'm all right. And I, um, I really need to see you. Right away."

There was a pause, a pure agony for Meggie. Then at last he asked warily, "See me about what?"

Meggie realized that her face was flaming. She laid her hand on her cheek in an attempt to cool the heat. It had been over a decade since that steamy Fourth of July night when she had thrown herself at him. She'd hardly spoken to him since. Still, she knew he must be wondering if she'd decided to try again—which, in a crazy way, was exactly the case.

"Look," she said, "I'd really prefer just to explain everything when I see you."

Another nerve-flaying silence occurred.

"Nate?" she asked faintly, fearing he might have hung up.

At last he spoke. "All right. One hour."

She felt breathless. She gulped in air. "Where?"

"The lobby."

"The lobby of what?"

"Your hotel."

Her hotel. That made sense. "All right, the lobby," she agreed. "Do you need the address?"

"I think I can find it," he said dryly.

"Well. All right." She confirmed the time. "In an hour then?" She got no reply. He'd already hung up.

Nate Bravo stood behind the ancient metal desk in his "office," which was really only a spare room in his apartment. His hand rested on the phone he'd just set down. He stared off toward the green bamboo blinds that covered the window. The blinds were rolled halfway up. Through the bottom half of the window, he could see the white stucco wall of the building next door. A hibiscus bush, blooming in lush explosions of coral pink, grew against that wall. A splash of sunlight made the green leaves shine and the white wall gleam. A pretty sight.

But Nate stared blindly, not really seeing the bright tropical flowers. His mind was filled with Meggie May Kane.

He could see her as if she stood before him, in Wranglers and a plaid shirt, her skeins of shining dark hair coming loose from under her hat, those big amber eyes staring at him with yearning—and a strange, defiant pride.

When he thought of Meggie May, he thought of contradictions. Of strength and innocence. Toughness and purity.

He was probably a damn fool to meet with her. What he wanted and what she wanted were worlds—universes—apart.

But then again, she'd sounded pretty upset. Just maybe she needed the kind of help he could provide: someone found. Or someone followed. He could do something like that for her. And he would. Willingly.

He found her sitting in a studded leather mission-style chair, wearing a sundress and sandals. Except for those strong, work-toughened hands gripping the chair arms, no one would have guessed that she was a woman who had pulled, cut and branded more than her share of calves. Her big eyes looked up at him, as pure and innocent as ever.

"Thank you. For coming." She stood and held out one of those calloused hands. He took it and they shook, awkward and formal. Then she cast a quick, uncomfortable glance around the lobby, with its Moorish arches, red-tiled floor and Persian rugs. A family sat in a group of leather chairs to their left, all dressed up for playing tourists, in shorts and sun visors, armed with cameras and binoculars. To their right, a man sat alone, reading the Sunday *Times*. And not far away, on a studded leather sofa, slouched four refugees from the punk scene, complete with safety pins in their ears and hair that went from Day-glo green to fluorescent purple. No one looked the least bit interested in the pretty woman in the sundress and the man who'd just shaken her hand.

Still, Meggie suggested, "Could we go on up to my room, do you think? Somewhere we could talk alone?"

Nate almost said no, since she had yet to tell him what the hell this was about. But then he scoffed at himself. What could Meggie May Kane do to him alone in her room that he couldn't handle?

They took the elevator up. In the enclosed space, Nate found himself overly conscious of her. Of her slightly woodsy perfume and those unwavering eyes, of the high roundness of her breasts beneath that pretty little dress. He had always found her physically attractive—which was why, from the time she started to fill out, he'd done his best to keep clear of her. A woman like Meggie, so rooted to the land, could never be anything but trouble to a man like him.

And really, by now, she should represent little to no threat to his peace of mind. All logic declared that physical attraction faded over time. Yet somehow, she still drew him. Now, in her early thirties, she seemed even more attractive than she had been in her teens. There was a lushness to her now, a ripeness she hadn't possessed before.

The elevator slid to a stop. The doors opened. She led the way down the hall to her room.

Once inside, she set her small purse on the round table in the corner, near a glass door that led out to a balcony. She gestured. "Have a seat." He walked past the end of the bed and dropped into the chair she'd offered. She indicated the small liquor cabinet not far away. "Can I get you something?"

"Why not? Jack Daniels. And ice."

He watched her as she got the key, unlocked the cabinet and took out the miniature bottle. The ice bucket was empty. She held it up. "I'll be right back."

He let her get to the door before he stopped her. "Never mind. I'll take it straight."

"Are you sure? It won't take a minute to get the ice."

"Straight is fine."

She returned to the small mirrored bar area over the liquor cabinet and poured him the drink. He nodded his thanks when she handed it to him, then lifted the glass and sipped, watching her over the rim as he did.

She stood unmoving for a moment, managing somehow to look both nervous and thoroughly self-possessed. She eyed the other chair, but must have decided against sitting in it, because she backed up until her knees hit the edge of the bed. She scooped the back of her dress smooth, then sat.

They regarded each other. In the silence, he became more aware of the noises from outside, of people laughing and talking from the pool area below the balcony, of a helicopter in the distance somewhere and the far-off scream of a siren. Just another day in paradise, he thought with some irony.

He glanced over at the balcony door. "You shouldn't leave that open. This isn't Medicine Creek." Medicine Creek was the small Wyoming town where they'd both gone to high school. Meggie still lived on a ranch not far from there. "In L.A. the burglars tend to be fast and agile."

"I'll close it next time I leave the room."

"And at night."

She shrugged. "Whatever."

Exasperation rippled through him—at himself for giving a damn whether she left her balcony door open or not. And at her, for smelling so good and looking so good. For the power of the attraction that still existed, against all logic, between them.

He sipped again from his drink, then set it on the table and stared at the small amount of amber liquid in the bottom of the glass. "What do you want from me, Meggie?"

He heard her shift on the bed. "My father died. A week ago today. Did you know?"

Nate shook his head. He still had family in Medicine Creek. But it had been a month or two since he'd talked to any of them. "I hadn't heard."

Meggie's hands gripped the edge of the bed, on either side of her thighs. She stared down at her own knees. "It was cancer. But he would never let Doc Pruitt look at him. He just got thinner and thinner. And then, for a few weeks, he got really sick. And then he died."

Nate reached for the drink again. "I'm sorry." He offered the bland condolence, not knowing what the hell else to say. He drank. Then, with finality, he set the glass down. He looked at her, waiting.

She coughed, as if her throat had gone tight on her. "This is hard."

"I'm listening."

"Um, well, it was just assumed that he'd leave me the Double-K."

Alarm had him sitting up a little straighter. "You mean he didn't?"

"No, he did. Sort of. With a couple of conditions."

"What conditions?"

With a small sigh, she rose, went to the closet nook and took some papers from her suitcase, which stood open on the rack below the hangers. Looking solemn, she returned to him.

Reluctantly, he took the papers from her hand.

"That's my father's will." She moved over so she

stood beside him. The woodsy smell of her taunted him as she pointed at the page on top. "Read from there."

He stared down at all the legal mumbo jumbo. "Look. Why don't you just explain it to me?"

He set the papers on the table by his empty glass.

She sighed again. "All right." She returned to the end of the bed, where she sat once more. For a moment, he felt some relief, because the scent of her faded a little with the distance. But the relief didn't last long.

"My father's been after me for years now to get married and give him some grandchildren. But I just never met the right guy." She paused. Her gaze slid away, then defiantly met his once more. "I mean, I didn't love any of the ones who asked. So I turned them down. And, well, it looks like my father decided to make sure I'd get a husband and some kids—from beyond the grave, if you know what I mean."

Nate did know what she meant—or at least he caught the general drift. And that made him long to bolt from the chair and head for the door.

But he hadn't heard her out yet. It seemed only right to give her that much. Somehow, he made himself sit still for the rest.

Meggie closed her eyes and rubbed her temples. Then she rested her hands on her knees. "This is the situation. According to my father's will, the ranch will be kept in trust, with me as the legal operator, for a period of two years. During that time, I am required to bear a child as a result of a lawful marriage."

His urge to get the hell out intensified. It was just as he'd feared. He asked, "And if you don't?"

"Then the Double-K will become public land."

"You'll get *nothing?*"

"Not exactly. My father set it up so that the herd will

be sold at auction and all proceeds from that auction will be mine. I'll also get the money from the sale of the home place, which includes the main house, the old bunkhouse where my cousin and his family live now, the homesteader's cabin and the outbuildings, including the forty acres those buildings stand on. With that, and the profits from the sale of the stock, my father figured I'd have enough for a fresh start.''

Nate found he could breathe a little easier. ''So you won't be destitute.''

''No. But I *will* lose the Double-K.''

''What I mean is, you'll end up with a decent chunk of change, anyway.''

Her generous mouth was a thin line. ''Without the Double-K, who cares?''

He'd had enough of circling the point. He said flatly, ''You called me here to ask me to marry you and try to get you pregnant.''

She just stared at him with those big, soulful eyes.

''Have I got it right?'' he demanded.

Very slowly, she nodded.

Nate stood. ''No.'' He headed for the exit.

She jumped up, zipped around him and plastered herself against the door. ''Nate. Just listen. Just give me—''

''Get away from the door.''

But she refused to budge. ''Nate. Please. You have to listen to me.''

If she'd been anyone else, he would have shoved her aside and gotten the hell out. But somehow, he couldn't bring himself to lay a hand on her.

''Nate.'' Her husky voice reached out, curled around him like smoke. ''I told you how I felt about you once. And you sent me away. And I never meant to bother you again. I swear to you. But I had two dreams, Nate. My ranch. And you. How can you ask me to give up both?''

"I'm not asking a damn thing of you."

She let out a tight, frantic-sounding laugh. "I know. You never have. And you never will...."

"Find someone else."

She pressed herself harder against the door, her eyes burning with a purposeful fire. "That's exactly what I intend to do. If you turn me down."

That gave him pause; he refused to think why.

She talked fast. "Listen. This is my offer. I'm not asking for a lifetime from you. I don't want to fence you in and I'm not asking you to settle down. I want a ring on my finger. And a baby. And as soon as the baby's born, we can get a..." She hesitated over the next word, but she did get it out. "Divorce."

"This is insane."

"Not for me. For me, it would be the best of a bad deal. Because at least my baby's father would be the man I love."

That spooked him good. He fell back a step.

She must have seen the panic in his eyes. She put up a hand. "It's just a fact, Nate. I don't expect it to mean a thing to you. I swear. I love you, have loved you and will always love you. And if I'm going to have a baby, I want it to be yours. I won't tie you down. Just a ring and a baby, and then you're free."

He shook his head. What she asked was so much like her: a total contradiction in terms. He spoke more kindly. "Meggie..."

"No. Listen. There's more."

"Meggie, this isn't going to—"

She ran right over him. "I have twenty thousand dollars that my grandmother Kane left to me. It's mine, free and clear. And I'll give it to you. As payment for…what I'm putting your through.''

His gut tightened all over again. Essentially, she had just offered to pay him for fathering her child. The thought sickened him.

She wasn't finished. "I will go on my knees to you, Nathan Bravo. I will do anything. Anything at all.''

"Stop."

She obeyed his command, waited there against the door, still begging with those big eyes.

He decided to try reason. "Look. Just slow down here. Let's just look logically at what you're asking.''

"Yes," she agreed eagerly. "Fine. Let's look at it logically.''

"Okay, then. What exactly are you thinking about here? Is this going to be some kind of test-tube thing?''

She stared. "What?''

"Are you talking about artificial insemination?''

Her face went crimson. She stammered, "Well, no. I mean, we would be married. And married people, um…''

"So you plan for us to have sex together?''

"Um. Well. Yeah.''

"The more sex the better, right? To increase the odds that you'll actually conceive.''

She frowned. "Yes. So?''

"Think. How are we going to do that, Meggie? I do have a life and a business to run—here, in L.A. I can't move to the Double-K for however long it takes you to get pregnant. And you can't run a ranch from my apartment.''

"We could work it out. I know we could. I've thought it through. You could stay at the Double-K as much as possible through the fall. Oh, I know you'd have to leave sometimes, when something just couldn't wait. But you're your own man, right? And we could it make a point to, um, get together at the most crucial times, when I'm...ovulating.''

Ovulating. Where the hell did they get words like that? "Meggie, listen—''

But she wouldn't listen. "No, really. It could work. It *will* work. And the money I'd pay you would help to make up for any business you might lose.''

Anger arrowed through him again at the mention of the money. "Forget the damn money.''

"No, really. I would want to pay you. I would want you to get something out of this for yourself.''

"I said, forget the damn money.'' It was a command.

She raised both hands, palms out. "All right. Whatever. But listen. We *could* work it out, so we could be together. You could stay with me as much as possible until the snows come. And then, when things get quiet at the ranch, Sonny and Farrah could handle things.''

"Sonny and Farrah?''

"My cousin and his wife. They work for me now, for the last three years or so.''

He thought he remembered hearing that somewhere. "Right.''

She rushed on. "Anyway, as soon as winter comes, I would come here and stay with you, until calving season. And with any luck, by then I'd be pregnant. You'd go back to your life and I'd go back to mine and when the baby comes, I'd send you the divorce papers in the mail. Okay?''

He only looked at her, shaking his head.

"Nate, please...''

He kept looking at her, showing her nothing—except

his refusal. And then he said it aloud. "No, Meggie. I just can't help you with this. Now, get out of my way."

"Nate…"

"I said, get out of my way."

That did it. He watched the hope fade from her eyes. "That's your final decision?"

He nodded.

"Oh, Nate…"

"Move aside."

She drew her shoulders back. "Fine. But I mean it. If you won't do it, I will find someone else."

He looked her up and down. "That's supposed to change my mind? Give me a break."

Give me a break.…

Those were the words he had said to her all those years ago, when she had told him she loved him.

"I love you," she had sworn. "And I will always love you."

He had looked down at her flushed face, at her full lips, which were soft and swollen from his kisses. And he had sneered, "Give me a break."

She hadn't forgotten, any more than he had. He could see it in her eyes.

Now, foolishly, he felt remorse. For hurting her again. For dimming the brightness of those beautiful eyes. "Meggie…" He reached out.

She ducked away, before he could touch her. And then she drew herself up once more. She turned and opened the door, stepping back, so the exit was clear. "Goodbye, Nate."

He had an idiot's urge to say more. But he quelled it.

With a final curt nod, he left her.

Chapter Two

Unfortunately, over the days that followed, Nate couldn't get Meggie out of his mind.

On Wednesday, three days after the meeting in her hotel room, he called his cousin Zach. Zach Bravo ran the family ranch, the Rising Sun Cattle Company, which shared more than one boundary with the Double-K. Zach and Meggie were good friends. When either came up shorthanded, the other would help out. The Kanes always put in an appearance during branding time at the Rising Sun. And there was usually a Bravo around if Meggie needed help in calving season.

Nate waited to call until nine at night, which was seven in Wyoming. By then, the day's work should be through and the dinner dishes cleared from the table.

Some strange woman answered the phone. "Yeah?"

Nate wondered if he'd dialed wrong. "Is this the Rising Sun?"

"Yeah."

"This is Nate. Nate Bravo?"

"Yeah, I heard of you."

"Let me talk to Zach."

"Hold on."

It took Zach forever to come on the line. Nate started to wonder if the strange woman had bothered to tell his cousin that he had a call. But finally, Nate heard the quiet, low voice.

"Hello, Nate."

"Hey, Zach."

"How are you doing?"

"Fine. Who the hell was that?"

Zach chuckled. "Mable LeDoux. She and her husband, Charlie, hired on about a month ago."

"She's keeping house and cooking?"

"You got it." Zach sounded grim. "And she's no Edna."

A year ago, Edna Heller, the ranch's longtime housekeeper, had become ill and been forced to retire. Edna had always taken care of the house—and the Bravos—as if they were her own. And the meals she used to put on the table, both in the main house and for the hands, kept everyone smiling. Zach was having a hell of a time trying to replace her. And it sounded as if Mable wouldn't last much longer than the others had.

Zach asked, "You coming home?"

"Not unless you need me."

"Nah, I'm dealing with things all right." Zach waited. He knew Nate. And Nate never called just to shoot the breeze.

Nate realized he probably should have thought this through a little better before picking up the phone.

"Nate? You okay?"

"Yeah. I'm fine. Listen. I heard that Meggie May's dad died."

Dead silence. Then Zach said, "Yeah. About a week and a half ago."

"How's she been?"

Another silence. Nate could almost hear Zach's mind working, as he carefully chose what to say. At last, he muttered grudgingly, "She's all right, I guess."

"You seen her much, since the funeral?"

More dead air. Then Zach said, "Meggie May's a good woman, Nate."

Damn. That was the thing about family. They always knew too much. "You don't have to worry about her and me," Nate said. "Nothing ever happened between us to speak of. And there's nothing going on now."

"Did she show up down there to see you?"

Nate muttered a word that would have made Edna Heller threaten to wash his mouth out with soap. "How did you know?"

"The Merchant's Society put on a dance, over at Medicine Creek Park, on the Fourth. I saw Meggie there. She asked about you."

"Asked what?"

"Asked if your name was in the L.A. phone book."

"What did you tell her?"

"I said, 'Bravo Investigative Services, in the Yellow Pages.' So. Did she come and see you?"

"Yeah, she came."

Another disapproving silence, then Zach asked, "Are you gonna tell me what this is all about?"

"No."

Zach grunted. "I don't think I like this."

"Don't worry, it's no big deal," Nate lied. Then he added, "I just need to know if she's all right."

"She's fine, last I heard. You remember that cousin of hers, Sonny? Used to come and stay over at the Double-K sometimes, in the summers?"

"Yeah."

"Well, Meggie and Sonny are running the Double-K together now."

"Yeah, I heard that."

"Sonny dropped by yesterday. Said they hired a new hand on Monday. Just temporary, Sonny says, until they get on top of things. I guess they fell behind some when Jason died."

A new hand. What did that mean? Did she plan to ask some no-account cowpuncher to father her child? "What do you know about him?"

"Who?"

"The new hand."

"Not a thing. Listen, Nate. That's all I can tell you. Because that's all I know. Last time I saw Meggie was on the Fourth. She seemed okay, for a woman whose dad had just died."

"Look..."

"What?"

He realized he didn't have anything worthwhile to say. So he muttered, "Hell. Nothing."

"Why don't you come on home for a while?" Zach suggested, more gently. "I'm not short of hands, but I can always use another pair. Lots of weeds to poison and ditches to burn. Not to mention hay to cut and fences to mend."

Nate felt the pull. He always did. If he closed his eyes, he could see the Big Horns, looming so high and proud over the endless, rolling prairie land. Overhead, there would be clean blue sky, with clouds like castles, white and high. And off to the east, a hawk soaring...

"Nate. What do you say?"

He remembered his freedom. He remembered his life. "Nah. Not right now."

"It *is* your place, too," Zach reminded him. Technically, the Rising Sun belonged equally to Nate and Zach and their third cousin, Cash. But Zach was the operator; he loved the ranching life and he made it pay.

"Some other time," Nate promised.

"I know, I know. Thanksgiving. Or Christmas. Don't let that L.A. smog fog your brain."

Nate promised he wouldn't and said goodbye.

He managed to hold off two more days before he got nuts enough to call Edna. Edna Heller was not only the former housekeeper of the Rising Sun, but also the mother-in-law of his other cousin, Cash. She could drive a man crazy, telling him what to eat and warning him to take care of himself, but Nate loved her anyway. She'd looked after him good, all those years ago, when his dad died and his mother turned him over to his grandpa Ross and took off for parts unknown. Edna had clucked over him and hugged him whether he liked it or not and generally treated him like a son, the way she'd done all three of the Bravo cousins. Widowed for two years now, Edna lived in a nice two-story house, which Cash had bought for her, in Medicine Creek.

And Edna always knew who was seeing whom.

"Why, it's funny you should ask about Megan May," Edna declared just a little too knowingly. "Because only this past Friday night Tillie Spitzenberger saw her at Arlington's Steak House with Barnaby Cotes. Kind of a surprise, everyone says, since we all thought she'd more or less told that boy she wasn't interested years ago...."

Edna chattered on, but Nate wasn't listening. Barnaby Cotes was the son of a Medicine Creek shop owner. And a smug, self-important piece of work if there ever was one. The thought of Cotes putting his slimy hands on Meggie made the blood pump too fast through Nate's veins. She deserved better than some fatheaded prig like that.

"Nathan, are you listening to me?"

"You know I am, Edna."

"Well then, what are you planning to do about Megan May?"

"Nothing."

"Then why did you ask about her?"

"Edna."

"Yes, Nathan?"

"Let's drop it."

"Always so prickly. When are you coming home? We miss you. And you should see that nephew of yours. He's getting bigger and better-looking every day. Just like his daddy." Cash's son, Tyler, had been born just the Christmas before. "Nathan?"

"I'm still here."

"Well? Are you coming home? We haven't seen you in months. It's too long. And I worry that you don't eat right, and it's bound to be dangerous, chasing after criminals and shady characters the way you do."

"I'm not planning to come home right now."

"When, then?"

"I can't say for sure."

She lectured him some more. And finally, about ten minutes later, he managed to say goodbye and get off the phone.

After that call, he swore to himself that he would make no more attempts to learn about Meggie May. He told himself that her search for a husband to father her child was none of his damn business, and promised himself he'd put her completely from his mind.

But then, on Monday, a week and a day after meeting with Meggie at the Hollywood Franklin, Nate got a job offer to track an embezzler down into Mexico. The money was right and expenses were generous. And still, he heard himself turning it down.

The new hand, Lev Jarvis, jumped out to open the gate and Sonny drove the pickup through. Lev walked the gate closed and sprinted over to join Sonny and Meggie.

Meggie leaned out the passenger window of the cab as a pair of grasshoppers leaped out from under the wheels, their wings snapping and shining in the sun. Meggie looked up at the blue bowl of the sky. The few clouds in sight looked like little shreds of white cotton. It was hot. Not far off, barn swallows hovered, ready to swing away after any hopper that dared to jump too high.

Meggie smiled to herself. She was happy to be out, doing useful work. The days really weren't so bad. It was the nights that killed her lately. Thinking of her home. And what she must do if she hoped to keep it.

But when she trundled around checking the stock with Sonny, she could tip her face to the sun and keep her mind on work. She glanced out over the pasture. It had been a pretty good year, with respectable rainfall. The grass still had green in it. And here and there, even now in July, she could still pick out the tiny bright heads of purple flax and the sunny faces of black-eyed Susans.

Lev, who was shy and respectful and young enough

not to fear skin cancer, took off his shirt and tossed it in the back of the pickup. Meggie grinned at him and pointed. "There's a pond over that ridge there. I figure there should be fifteen heifers and their first calves hanging around it. We'll check the salt box and the mineral tubs." They'd also check the stock. They'd look for heifers with tight bags, which would mean a calf wasn't sucking. They'd search for any sick animals, which they'd take home to treat. They'd look over the calves for any sores. In the heat, a calf could be dead in a day or two from an untreated wound. And they'd hope to find only the Black Angus bulls they'd put in that pasture last month. Black Angus bulls produced a small, wiry calf that hit the ground running. They were the perfect bulls to put with heifers, both in their first and second years of calving out, because a smaller calf made for an easier birth.

"Hop in," Meggie said.

Lev joined his shirt in the back of the pickup. Sonny shifted into gear, but he didn't get ten feet before a horn honked, loud and long, behind them at the pasture gate. Sonny put on the brakes. Meggie leaned farther out her window and looked back.

It was one of the Bravo pickups. That big old GMC that Nate's grandfather Ross used to favor in the final years before he died. Meggie squinted, trying to see through the glare on the windshield to whoever was behind the wheel. But she couldn't make out the face.

She swung open her door. "I'll be right back." She sprinted toward the GMC. At the gate, she paused to slip the latch and slide through. As soon as she got past the glaring windshield and looked in the open window of the driver's door, she saw the man behind the wheel.

Her poor heart started thundering so loud she felt sure all of Johnson County could hear it.

She froze a few feet from the door and put her hand to her throat. "What?" she asked. The word sounded as numb and dazed as she felt.

Nate hung an elbow out the driver's door, looking perfectly casual, as if he drove out to her ranch in his granddaddy's old pickup every day of the week. "Your cousin's wife said I might find you here."

She gaped at him. She had absolutely no idea what to say. Stalling, trying to get her wits back about her, she took off her hat, fiddled with the brim for a moment, then put it back on.

Nate looked past her "Who's that?" He nodded at the pickup that still waited for her in the pasture beyond the gate.

She looked where he nodded. "Who?"

"That fool with his shirt off." He sounded angry.

"That's Lev. Lev Jarvis. He hired on to help out for a while."

"Doing what?" His tone was nasty.

Meggie saw no point at all in replying to that, so she didn't.

"Get in," he said.

"Why?"

"We have to talk."

She looked toward the other pickup again. "Now?"

"Now."

Meggie considered. It wasn't exactly the perfect time for a talk. Evening would have been better, after the day's work was through. But hope had lit a fire inside her again. Why else would he show up here, but to tell her that he had changed his mind about her request?

She'd go insane waiting till evening to hear what he had to say.

"Well?"

"Wait here." She turned and slid back through the gate.

"What's going on?" Sonny asked when she reached the driver's side of the cab.

"It's Nate Bravo." She knew she sounded breathless, but that was no big deal. After all, she had been running.

Sonny, who was tall, thin, sandy haired and pretty much like a brother to her, frowned at her through his open window. "Nate Bravo? What the hell's he doing here?"

Guilt poked at her. Meggie had yet to say a word to Sonny about the will. As far as he knew, he and Farrah and their two kids had a place to live and work for as long as they wanted it. She'd already lied to him outright about the situation once, when she'd told him she had to go down to Cheyenne to see about a certain Black Angus bull—when in reality, she'd booked a flight to L.A. She hated to lie, but she wanted to have some kind of solution to the problem before she told him about it.

And just maybe, today, Nate would give her a solution.

"Meggie, what's Nate Bravo doing here?" Sonny asked again.

She avoided the question. "I want to talk to him for a while. You and Lev go on over to the pond without me, okay?"

"You're going off with Nate Bravo?" Sonny sounded thoroughly disapproving. Nate had always had a bad reputation. Apparently even Sonny, who had only lived in the area for the past few years, had heard the rumors about him, about how wild he'd been while growing up, and how he'd always sworn he would never settle down.

"Like I said, I need to talk to him. And I'm not sure how long it's going to take. I'll just have to catch up with you."

Sonny was quiet for a moment, then he asked, "Is something going on that I should know about?"

Meggie forced a confident smile. "No. It's nothing." Guilt nudged her again. It was a lot more than nothing. But she certainly couldn't be expected to explain it all now.

Sonny studied her face for a long moment before he nodded. "We'll check the Deerling pasture after we're through here." He referred to the next pasture north. They called it the Deerling pasture because Meggie's father had bought it from the Deerlings when old man Deerling died and his family had to sell it to pay the inheritance taxes. The Deerlings had sold out altogether not long after that and moved to Oregon. But they still had a pasture in Wyoming named after them.

"Go on." Meggie slapped the door of the pickup. Sonny saluted her and shifted into gear again. She stood, watching, until the pickup crested the rise and disappeared on the other side.

Then she turned and ran back to where Nate waited for her.

Nate drove too fast. They bounced over the rutted dirt road as if one of the bad guys he chased for a living had turned the tables and come after him for a change. Meggie held on to the "chicken" handle over the door and didn't say a word. Finally, he jerked the wheel to the side and pulled off into a patch of sage and buffalo grass. He switched off the engine and draped an arm over the top of the steering wheel.

He stared out the windshield at the rolling prairie that went on forever up ahead. "Have you made your offer to any other men?"

She looked straight ahead, too. "No."

Actually, she had tried to make herself ask Barnaby Cotes. She'd run into him in town last week, and said yes when he invited her to dinner. But an evening with him had reminded her too thoroughly of all the ways he wasn't Nate. And somehow, though she knew she must find a husband, she just hadn't quite managed to make herself propose to Barnaby.

"What about Barnaby Cotes?" Nate demanded.

She blinked and looked at him, wondering if he had read her mind. "Who told you I went out with Barnaby?"

He still didn't look at her, but the side of his mouth twisted with irony. "I'm a detective, remember?"

She figured it out. "You called Edna."

He grunted, still looking out the window. "Yeah. I called Edna." He fisted his hand and tapped it on the steering wheel. "So. Did you tell Cotes? About the will? About what you need?"

"No, I did not."

She kept looking at his profile, at his hawklike nose and his high cheekbones, at his straight black hair that he always left just long enough to make him look disreputable. His mother, Sharilyn Tickberry Bravo, was part Lakota Sioux. And the mark of his ancestors was strong in Nate's face—on both sides. He had cheekbones like knife blades, a nose fit for a tribal chief and the Bravo mouth, which was a little bit full for a man. A mouth that looked like it was made to kiss a woman.

"Who knows about this, Meggie?" Nate demanded.

She kept her head high. "You, me and G. Vernon Bannister."

"Who's G. Vernon Bannister?"

"The lawyer who handled my father's will."

"No one else?"

"Why does it matter?"

He continued to stare out the bug-spattered windshield. Then at last he said, "I guess it doesn't matter. I just wanted to know, that's all."

"Well, G. Vernon Bannister told me. And I told you. And that's as far as it's gone."

"Fine."

"And now it's my turn to ask a question."

"Ask."

"Why are you here?"

He turned to look at her then. His dark eyes were hard and fathoms deep. "I changed my mind. I'll marry you."

Chapter Three

Meggie found she couldn't speak.

But it didn't matter, because Nate had more to say. "If the offer's still open, I'll accept your proposition pretty much as you laid it out a week ago—with a couple of conditions."

She managed to croak, "Name them."

He did. "You agree from the first that if I do give you the child you need, I'll always be free to see him. He'll also be allowed to come stay with me whenever I can make decent arrangements for his care."

Meggie saw nothing wrong with that. "Agreed."

He added, "And I won't take any money from you, period."

She couldn't go along with that. It just didn't seem fair. Even though he'd never said the words, she knew in her heart that Nate cared for her in his own independent way. He understood how much the Double-K meant to her. And in the end, he was coming through to help her keep it. She wanted to pay him back for that, somehow.

"Nate, really. It's silly for you to be so stubborn about—"

"No money."

"But you should be getting *something* out of—"

He glared at her. "No money."

It was hot in the cab of that pickup. Meggie took off her hat and armed sweat from her forehead. "I'm not exactly in a position to argue with you." She tossed her hat on the seat between them. "So you just go right ahead and cheat yourself." Freed of the hat, her hair started falling down.

A hint of a grin came and went on Nate's mouth. "Thanks. I will."

Meggie twisted her hair tight again and anchored it more securely at the back of her head. She smoothed the last stray hairs into place.

She felt guilty, to be giving in on this issue. But the hard truth was, she needed that money. If everything went as she prayed it would, she'd have some hefty inheritance taxes to pay in two years. She didn't want to end up like the Deerlings, with someone else's pasture named after her. She wanted to keep her ranch. Now, with Nate's help, she just might manage that.

"Okay, then. That's settled," she said. "You get no money."

"Good enough." He was grinning again.

She couldn't help grinning right back. "So. Have I met all your terms?"

"You sure have."

They stared at each other, across the seat of the cab. Only her hat lay between them. She could have moved it. Or they could have leaned across it, to share the kiss that would seal this strange marriage bargain. But they didn't.

As Meggie gazed into those dark eyes, a memory came to her. Of the first time she ever saw him, the summer they were both fourteen—the summer Nate's grandfather had brought him to live at the Rising Sun.

Nate had been nothing but trouble to his grandpa that first year. And the day Meggie met him was no exception. He'd stolen a Rising Sun pickup that day, a pickup not much different from the one he and Meggie sat in now. And he'd gone joyriding on the rutted dirt roads that crisscrossed his grandpa's ranch.

Probably without even realizing it, he'd crossed over onto Double-K land. The muffler of the pickup must have been scraping the road ruts, setting off sparks. The sparks found dry grass.

Meggie had been lying just over a rise, next to Crystal Creek, naked, after a refreshing swim. Her favorite horse, a sorrel gelding she'd named Renegade, nipped the grass nearby. Renegade had lifted his head and sniffed the air. And then he'd let out a long, nervous whinny. Meggie looked up and saw the smoke—just a tiny trail of it. But on the prairie, a tiny wisp of smoke could become an inferno in no time at all.

She yanked on her underpants, her boots and her shirt, jumped into the saddle and took off. Over the rise, she rode up on a black-haired boy. He'd just managed to beat out the flames with an old blanket he must have found in the truck.

He looked up at her, his face smudged and his eyes wild—and then he burst out laughing. "You're damn near naked!" he crowed.

She called him a fool. An idiot. A jerk. And then she

started laughing, too. It was good, to laugh like that with someone. She and her father lived alone at the ranch, except for the hired hands that came and went. Jason Kane wasn't much of a talker, so Meggie sometimes found herself tongue-tied in company.

But she didn't feel tongue-tied with this boy. She sensed a kinship with him. She just knew that here was a friend. And she suspected that he knew it, too.

"Wait here," she told him when the laughter finally faded. "I'll go put my clothes on."

When she returned, he was still there. She gave him a hand up and he rode behind her, back to the creek again. He slid down from Renegade and knelt at the bank to wash the soot from his face and to drink long and deep. She dismounted, too, and joined him. They ended up splashing each other, laughing some more.

And then, for at least an hour, they sat there, on the bank, in the shade of the cottonwoods, with the cottonwood fluff like fairy dust blowing in the incessant wind.

He told her who he was. And that his dad had died a few months before—of blood poisoning from not bothering to get himself a tetanus shot after some tough character had bitten him in a bar fight. Once they put his dad in the ground, Nate's mom had dumped him on his grandfather. Nate said he hated his grandfather, who was always looking at him sideways and shaking his head. Nate just knew that Ross Bravo wondered why he'd let someone like Nate come and live at his precious ranch. Nate also hated Edna Heller, who had decided to civilize him. And he couldn't stand his cousin Cash, who was perfect. And he despised his cousin Zach, who did everything right.

Meggie listened and nodded. She'd seen in Nate's eyes that he didn't really hate the Bravos and Edna. In time, he would realize he was one of them, too. And then things would be all right for him at the Rising Sun.

When they parted, Nate promised to meet her for a swim the next day. But he didn't show up. Ross grounded him, for stealing the pickup. Meggie didn't see him for weeks. But it didn't matter. They were friends.

Their friendship lasted for two years. Until they both started to grow up. Nate's shoulders broadened and he put on muscle. Meggie began to fill out, too. And boys started looking at her the way men looked at women. But Meggie had no interest in just any boy. Her eyes turned to Nate, and she saw more than a friend. At the same time, Nate started dating the girls a guy only went out with for one reason—and avoiding Meggie whenever they met, as if he didn't even know her anymore.

Meggie always thought of that period as the first time he broke her heart. The second time occurred a few years later, on that Fourth of July night, when she'd finally worked up the courage to tell him of her love—and he had scorned her.

Now, in the sweltering cab of Ross Bravo's old pickup, Meggie couldn't help wondering if she had just set herself up for heartbreak number three.

Nate began laying out alternatives for the wedding. "We could fly to Reno right away, I guess. Or I suppose we could go into the clinic in town tomorrow, get the blood tests and then get married at the county courthouse as soon as the results come in."

All at once, another problem occurred to her. A very delicate problem. One she'd promised herself she would face when she came to it. "Nate?"

"Yeah?"

"Um, there's something more I think we really should consider."

"What?"

"What if one of us…can't have children?"

He let out a long breath, then he picked up her hat from between them on the seat. He smoothed dual creases in the crown. "I have a suggestion."

"I'm listening."

"There's only so much you can do here. And then you just have to let nature take its course." He held out her hat.

She took it, put it on her head. "You're right. I know. But…"

"But what?" He sounded grim.

"Well, I think we should be realistic here. I need a baby. And I want to be as sure as I *can* be, going into this, that it's going to work."

"Get to the point Meggie."

"The point is…"

He stared at her, one of those hard, dark, unreadable stares of his.

She made herself say it. "Um, would you be willing to take a few tests?"

For a moment, he went on staring at her. Then he swore crudely under his breath. "You don't ask much, do you, Meggie May?"

She turned her body toward him, hoisted a leg up on the seat and rested her hand on the ankle of her boot. "Let's be frank, okay?"

He squinted at her disbelievingly. Then, with a snort, he shoved open his door, braced it with a boot and muttered, "It's hotter than the south end of hell in here."

Wisely, she refrained from pointing out that he was

the one who had chosen the cab of a truck in the middle of the prairie at midday in July to have this conversation. "Nate. Is there any possibility at all that you might want to…stay married to me, after this is all over and done?"

He was staring out the windshield again. Slowly, he faced her. "None."

She told herself that didn't hurt. "Okay. Then there's really no sense in putting ourselves through this if I'm infertile or you can't…father a child. Please. We're better off knowing where we stand."

He shook his head. "A few tests. You want me to take a few tests…."

Two days later, they drove to Billings together in Nate's rental car. Meggie had arranged appointments for them at a fertility clinic there. They sat in the waiting room for an hour, filling out forms.

Then they went in for an interview with the doctor.

Meggie explained their situation. They'd come to the clinic for a little assurance—in advance. They wanted to get married, but having children was a high priority for both of them. If there were any barriers to conception, Meggie hoped the doctor might discover them. "So we'll know where we stand on this right from the first," she said.

The doctor coughed into his hand. "Miss Kane. Most couples don't even contact a fertility specialist until they've been trying to conceive a child for at least a year."

"I understand that," Meggie replied carefully. "And I…respect that. I do. But Nate and I really want to know ahead of time if anything is going to keep us from being parents. It's just…terribly important to us."

The doctor frowned. "My dear young woman, even if I found no contraindications of fertility in either of you, there could still be a number of reasons conception might not occur. I am simply not in the business of providing guarantees."

Meggie rushed to reassure him. "Doctor, really. We aren't asking for a guarantee. Not at all. We just want help in ruling out the obvious."

"The obvious?"

"I mean, if either of us can absolutely *never* have children, we want to know."

The doctor looked at Nate. "And just where do you stand in this, Mr. Bravo?"

Nate slid a glance at Meggie and saw her smile grow tight. He knew she didn't feel she could count on him to back her up. And that inspired a perverse desire to prove her wrong.

He reached out and took her hand. She stiffened at the contact, but only a little—not enough that the doctor would notice. Nate brought her fingers to his lips and looked over her knuckles into her slightly panicked eyes. "Meggie wants me to give her a baby," he said to the doctor, though he didn't break contact with those wide brown eyes. "And I want Meggie to have what she wants."

"Do *you* want children yourself, Mr. Bravo?" the doctor inquired.

He lowered Meggie's hand, but he didn't let go of it. Instead, he twined his fingers with hers. "Absolutely." He rested their clasped hands in his lap and gave the doctor a big smile. "I want a whole houseful of kids. It's my major dream in life, to tell you the truth."

The doctor beamed back at him. "A real family man."

"I'm afraid you've found me out."

The doctor beamed some more. And then he coughed again. "Well then. All right. I think we can perform a few basic tests, though of course you'll each have to sign a release stating your understanding of the issues we've just discussed."

"Thank you," Nate said. He squeezed Meggie's hand, and she immediately tried to tug free. He didn't let her go. Instead, he smiled at her adoringly. "Say thank-you to the doctor, darling."

He saw the confusion in her eyes. He had surprised her, by playing along so well. And she wasn't sure if she liked it. But she didn't let him throw her. "Yes, Doctor. Thank you," she said with great sincerity. "Really. I can't tell you how much this means to me."

They went to separate rooms for their physicals. Nate's was strictly routine. The doctor measured his blood pressure and heart rate. He thumped Nate's chest and back, checked his reflexes with a little steel hammer, poked at his stomach and prodded his privates. As soon as the doctor left the examining room, a nurse came in and drew blood.

And then the nurse led Nate to the rest room at the end of the hall. She handed him a plastic cup. "We'll need a semen sample."

"Gotcha."

"We have a selection of men's magazines, if you think they might help."

"No, thanks. I'll manage."

Nate took his cup and entered the rest room, where he conjured up a nice little fantasy—centering around Meggie, as a matter of fact. It worked out fine.

The doctor spoke to them once more before they left,

informing them that the lab results should be back within forty-eight hours. They should make an appointment for another consultation.

The one hundred fifty–mile drive home didn't take that long, since Nate had the wheel and Montana had no speed limits. Meggie was silent for half of the ride. She stared out the window at the rolling land and the rows of drift fences positioned at a slant on the rises near the road, to catch the snow and control where it piled up.

Finally, she turned to him. "You were very convincing, with the doctor."

He shot her a single glance. "You're mad at me."

He saw her shrug in his side vision. "No," she said. "I admit you confused me. I don't think I've ever seen you so enthusiastic about anything, in all the years I've known you." She smiled out the windshield. "Actually, I kind of liked it."

Irritation rose in him. "It was only an act."

"I know that." She gave a soft little sigh and said no more.

He drove faster. They crossed into Wyoming. From the border, it didn't take long before he was pulling into the yard in front of the Double-K ranch house.

Meggie turned to him. "Monday, then? Early?"

"I'll be here to get you at eight. Is that early enough?"

"That's fine." She leaned on her door, climbed out and then paused before she shut it. "Nate?"

"Yeah?"

"Thanks. You were great. You really were."

A ridiculous flush of pleasure washed through him. He scowled at her. "You're welcome."

Still smiling that wide, gorgeous smile, she shut the door.

The next day was Friday. Nate spent it and the weekend that followed helping Zach out around the Rising Sun and avoiding his cousin's probing, suspicious glances. Zach knew something was up. But he'd never been a man who would pry. He'd wait for the right opening before he'd ask any questions. Nate made sure he got no openings.

Edna, however, never required openings. She considered the private lives of the Bravo cousins her own personal territory. And as soon as she learned that Nate had appeared at the Rising Sun, she insisted he and Zach must come to her place in town for Sunday dinner. Edna's housemate, Tess DeMarley, would cook.

The last time Nate had come home, over Christmas, Tess had cooked all the meals out at the ranch. Each one had been excellent. Nate looked forward to sampling her cooking again.

He did not, however, look forward to Edna's questions, which started the minute he and Zach walked in the door.

"Nathan." She hugged him and kissed him. "Come in. Sit down. And tell me. What's brought you home to us when it isn't even a holiday?"

"I just felt like a visit."

"Are you sure that's all? You were seen driving through town this past Thursday. With Megan May Kane."

"He was?" Zach glowered.

"Who saw me?" Nate demanded.

Edna patted his arm. "I'm sorry, Nathan. But I can't tell you that. Everyone knows about your temper. If someone was hurt because I opened my big mouth, well I simply could not live with myself.''

"I'm not going to hurt anyone, Edna."

"I just don't think it's wise for me to say any more."

"Well, your source is mistaken," Nate lied—with authority, he hoped.

Edna smiled indulgently. "My source is not mistaken. And here's Tess with that wonderful cheese ball of hers. You boys help yourselves, now."

They sat down to eat half an hour later. With Zach glaring at him and Edna watching him like a hawk, Nate found it hard to give the great food the attention it deserved. Tess's little daughter, Jobeth, eased the situation somewhat. She'd been out to the ranch a number of times and fallen in love with the place. She had a thousand questions for Zach—everything from how all the barn cats were doing to whether he'd seen her favorite bull snake in the cake shack lately. At least Zach stopped giving Nate dirty looks long enough to answer Jobeth's questions.

But the ride home was grim and deathly silent.

Once they got in the house, Zach turned to him. "You got anything you want to say to me?"

Now, how the hell could a man answer that? Nate lifted a shoulder in a careless shrug. "Not a thing."

Zach looked at him, a long look full of pained disapproval. And then he turned for the stairs.

Nate watched his cousin go, still wondering what he should have told him. It would have been jumping the gun to say that he and Meggie were getting married. She wanted to know the results of those tests they'd taken before they told anyone. And besides, at its core, the marriage was hardly the kind of arrangement Zach would approve of. Nate realized that he and Meggie had to talk; they had to decide exactly how much everyone would know about this marriage of theirs.

As agreed, they drove to Billings early the next day. There they learned that Nate was perfectly capable of fathering a child and that all of Megan's equipment appeared to be in working order, as well.

On the ride home, Meggie told Nate that the next step should be explaining the situation to her cousin Sonny. "He doesn't understand why I keep taking off with you."

Nate grunted. "He's heard about how bad I am, right?"

She sighed. "Oh, Nate…"

"Hey. It's no big deal. I *am* bad. And you shouldn't be hanging around with me."

"You are not bad."

"Am so."

They shared a glance, then he turned his gaze toward the road again. She said, "Seriously. Lately, it seems that every time I look at Sonny, I see worry in his eyes. And he does have a right to know what's going on."

"Fine. So tell him."

She shifted in her seat a little, and he knew she was building up to laying something new on him.

"Go on, spit it out," he said.

For a moment, she didn't say anything. He shot her another glance and saw she was looking out the passenger window, in the direction of a flock of blackbirds perched in close-packed rows on a drift fence that ran along a rise above the highway. It was rare to see so many of them together, this time of year. Usually, they spread out in the spring and didn't gather again until time for the fall migration. And yet, there they were, in the middle of summer, a whole flock of them. Before the car passed them, the birds took flight, like a hundred tiny ink spots scattered on the wind.

"Meggie. Speak."

"I'm trying. I've just, well, I've been thinking, that's all."

"Sounds dangerous."

"Don't tease."

"Sorry. 'You've been thinking...'"

"Well, I think we should let Sonny—and everyone else, too—believe this is a real marriage, not one with a built-in divorce at the end of it. I think it'll be easier on everyone if we just play it out as if we plan for it to last forever."

"And when the time comes to call it quits?"

"We'll just say it didn't work out."

Nate thought of Edna and the disapproving stares she could lay on a man. And he thought of Zach, so moral and upright. And Cash, who until pretty recently had been a lot like Nate—determined never to let some woman get control of his heart. But now Cash and Abby were as good as joined at the hip, and Cash had suddenly developed a lot of respect for the state of matrimony.

Nate could read the writing on the bathroom wall, all right. He would get no peace from anyone in his entire family if they knew he was playing temporary husband and sperm donor to Meggie May Kane.

"Nate?" Meggie asked nervously. "What do you say?"

"That I've been thinking along the same lines myself."

"Really?" She sounded genuinely relieved. "Terrific.'' She laid her arm along the back of the seat. "What do you think about the will?"

"What do you mean, what do I think?"

"I mean, should I tell Sonny and Farrah about it?"

"What for?"

"Well, they have a right to know, don't they, that I may lose the Double-K? It is their livelihood, too, after all."

"Hell. I suppose so."

"Good, then." She leaned toward him a little, across the seat. He got a whiff of that scent of hers—and he knew another request was coming at him.

"What else?" he demanded bleakly.

"I think you should be there when I tell them. You know. As my fiancé, it's only logical that you would be there at my side, giving me the love and support I need at a time like this."

"Right."

"I think you should come for dinner. About six tonight. Oh, and I want to give them a percentage of the Double-K, too—in the end, I mean, if everything works out. I thought I'd tell them about that tonight, along with everything else."

"It's your ranch."

"So that means you'll be there?"

He glared at the road ahead.

"Nate? Will you be there?"

Grudgingly, he muttered, "All right."

That night, in the old-fashioned kitchen of the Double-K ranch house, after dinner had been served and cleared off, Lev Jarvis returned to his quarters in the homesteader's cabin out beyond the corrals and the horse pasture. Farrah took her little son and daughter back across the yard to the old bunkhouse, which Sonny had fixed up into a home for his family.

Twenty minutes later, Farrah returned alone. She took the chair beside her husband, across the table from Meggie and Nate.

"Okay," Sonny said. "Suppose you tell us what is going on around here."

Meggie had the will ready. She stood and laid it before her cousin and his wife. "Read that section there."

Sonny and Farrah bent over the page. Then, after a few minutes, Sonny looked up. "This is some kind of condition that you have to fulfill to keep the Double-K, right?"

Meggie nodded. "I have to marry and have a baby within two years—or we lose the ranch."

Sonny and Farrah both frowned, then bent over the page again. At last, Sonny shoved the will away. "Are you sure?"

"Positive."

"Why the hell would he do a thing like that?"

Farrah put her hand over his. "Sonny…" she murmured soothingly.

"He's lucky he's dead," Sonny muttered. "If he wasn't, I'd kill him myself."

"Hush, now." Farrah squeezed his hand. "Don't speak ill of the dead."

"I'm sorry, Sonny," Meggie said. "I know I should have told you sooner. I just…I didn't know how to break it to you."

Sonny met her eyes. "What could have been in his mind? You meant everything to him. How could he do this to you?"

"He wanted me to get married. And have a family."

"Well, this is sure one crazy way to make that happen."

"I agree."

"We'll have to see a lawyer. We'll have to—"

Meggie was shaking her head. "I've checked into it. There's no breaking that will. Dad was sane. And he had a right to do whatever he wanted with what belonged to him. He had a lawyer draw that will up, and it's properly witnessed, too."

"So that means…"

"I fulfill the conditions—or we lose the ranch. Period."

Sonny groaned. "So what happens now?" And then his eyes shifted to Nate. The truth dawned. He looked at his cousin again. "Him?" he breathed in complete disbelief. "You're marrying *Nate Bravo?*"

Nate, who'd been pointedly ignoring the other man's dirty looks all evening, had to remind himself to keep cool. This was Meggie's show, after all. And he would let her run it however she saw fit. He would not lose his temper just because her uptight cousin considered him a bad marriage risk.

Hell, he *was* a bad marriage risk! So what was there to get offended about?

Meggie jumped right in to defend her choice. She reached for his hand and when she found it, she held on tight. "The truth is, I've always loved Nate."

Across the table, Sonny let out a snort of disbelief. He focused narrowed blue eyes on Nate. "You're some kind of detective in L.A., aren't you?"

"Yeah."

"So I don't get it. You live in L.A. Meggie lives here. How are you gonna get together to…uh…" His face turned as red as his hair.

Meggie swiftly explained that Nate would stay at the Double-K until fall. "And this winter, I'll have to ask you and Farrah to handle things here while I go to L.A."

Sonny looked totally unconvinced. "Right. And what about after that? Are you trying to tell us that every year the two of you will disappear to L.A.? You're planning to be a part-time rancher—is that what you're trying to say? There's no such thing, and we all know it."

Meggie's face turned red. "No. Of course I don't mean that, Sonny."

"Well, then, what do you mean?"

"I mean that…well, after this year, we'll have a better grip on everything. And we can…decide what to do next."

Meggie's half-baked, stammered explanation didn't convince Sonny of anything—except exactly what they'd been trying to keep him from figuring out. "I get it. You've made some deal with him. He'll marry you and try to give you…what you need. And after that, it won't matter who lives where, because you won't be together anyway."

"Oh, Sonny, no. You don't understand." Meggie looked miserable.

"What are you paying him?" Sonny demanded. "Your twenty thousand from Granny Kane?"

Nate decided it was time he stepped in. He held Meggie's hand tighter. "She's not paying me a damn thing."

Sonny blinked. "I'm not talking to you."

"Fine. But *I'm* talking to *you*. And I'm telling you that this is a real marriage." He spoke with outraged conviction, managing to sound as if he meant every word. "And Meggie and I plan for it to last the rest of our lives."

Sonny gaped, but still tried to keep up the cynicism. "Right. Sure."

"Bet on it. Come next spring, Meggie and I will be moving back here to stay." Where were all these lies coming from? Nate wondered vaguely—and then lied some more. "The truth is, this winter, while Meggie and I are in L.A., I'll be closing up my business there for good." As if there were a damn thing to close up, besides a two-bedroom apartment and a few utility bills.

Sonny took the bait. "You will?"

"Yeah. And once that's done, we'll be back here. Forever. Got that?"

Sonny gulped. "Well, yeah."

Nate looked Meggie's cousin up and down, then challenged, "So what do you think?"

"Uh, it sounds..."

"Good." Farrah provided the word for her floundering husband. "It sounds real good. If Meggie loves you and you love her, then we're happy for you both."

"And there's more," Meggie piped up.

She must mean the percentage she wanted to promise them. Nate gave her the floor. "Right. Meggie, tell them what you have planned."

Meggie gave him a look of pure adoration. Then she smiled at her cousin and his wife. "As soon as the terms of the will are met, Nate and I want to go into a real partnership with you two."

"A partnership?" Sonny looked a little dazed.

"Yes," Meggie said. "If everything works out, and Nate and I have the baby we need to keep the Double-K, I intend for you two to have a twenty-five-percent share of the place."

"No, Meggie…" Now Sonny looked stunned.

"Don't argue. You've worked hard for the Double-K for three years now. And you'll have to run things yourselves this winter. You deserve to be working for something you can call your own. When all this trouble is through, this will be partly your ranch, too. We'll all be in this together, in the best and truest sense." She turned her wide smile briefly on Farrah, and then focused on her cousin again. "So, what do you say?"

"I…Meggie, are you sure?"

"I am. Now, please. Make your peace with Nate, because the two of you will be working together from now on."

Sonny nodded. "All right." He met Nate's eyes. "I guess maybe I…jumped the gun a little."

Nate shrugged. "Forget it."

"No. The truth is, I heard a few things about you. That you were a wild kid. And not the kind of man who would ever be settling down. And I judged you on rumor. I can see now that I was wrong."

Nate felt about two inches high. Simple, hardworking men were always too damn easy to deceive. Still, the agreement he and Meggie had made was just between the two of them. He would keep up the act. He held out his hand. "Let's start fresh from here."

They shook across the table.

"You take good care of her," Sonny warned.

"I will," Nate promised. That wasn't a total lie. He *would* take good care of Meggie. He would give her what she needed to keep what she loved. And then, as her cousin had guessed before Nate started conning him, they would go their separate ways.

Chapter Four

Nate and Meggie said their vows that Saturday, at the Johnson County Courthouse in Buffalo, with Sonny and Farrah as witnesses. They planned to drive back to Medicine Creek, stop for dinner at Arlington's Steak House and then head on home to the ranch. Meggie walked out of the courthouse on her new husband's arm, feeling happy and full of hope—almost as if she and Nate had just married for real and forever. The sun shone down from a cloudless sky.

They didn't get five steps along Main Street before Cash, the blond, blue-eyed charmer of the Bravo cousins, pulled up beside them in his Cadillac. He slid across the seat and shoved open the back door. "Get in."

"What the hell is this?" Nate demanded.

"A kidnapping, what do you think?" Cash met his

cousin's dark stare. "So just do what I tell you—for once. Or there will be hell to pay."

"Says who?"

"Edna."

Nate turned to Meggie, a sheepish grin on his face. "If Edna wants us, then I guess we'd better go."

Meggie laughed. "Fine by me."

Nate took her elbow to help her into the car. But then he stopped and looked around. "What happened to Sonny and Farrah and the kids?"

"They're already on their way where we're going," Cash said. "Now, get in. We were supposed to be there ten minutes ago."

Cash took them to Medicine Creek—but not to Arlington's Steak House. Instead, he delivered them to the big house he shared with Abby and their son on North Street.

"March up to the door and knock," he commanded.

They did as they were told. Edna Heller answered, all dressed for a party in a blue silk shirtwaist, looking so dainty and feminine it was hard to believe that she possessed a will of iron and the relentless determination of a drill sergeant.

"Oh, here you both are, at last." Edna kissed Meggie. "Oh, my dear. I am so thrilled about this." She held out her arms to Nate, who obediently moved in for a hug. "Congratulations, Nathan." She patted his broad back. "You are a very lucky man."

She stepped back, beaming, and turned to lead them into the high-ceilinged living room.

Friends and family were waiting there. In unison, everyone shouted, "Surprise!"

Abby stepped right up, her pretty face alight and her blond hair, as usual, falling in her eyes. She grabbed

Meggie and hugged her. "I said this would happen," she whispered in Meggie's ear.

"You did?"

"Yep. Last year. On my own wedding day."

Meggie had no time to respond to that, because Zach grabbed her, spun her off the floor and hugged her hard. She was passed from embrace to embrace. It felt wonderful.

After all the hugging was through, Meggie looked around in delight. Cash and Abby had spared no expense. They'd hired a caterer from Sheridan, the same one, Abby whispered, who'd put on their own wedding reception—in this very house, the year before. An array of tempting dishes waited on white-clothed tables and the bar had been fully stocked. The caterer had also brought along a four-piece band.

"Oh, you really shouldn't have." Meggie sighed.

"Oh, yes, we should," Abby shot back. "Now, get out on that floor and dance."

Meggie didn't hesitate. She danced with Zach and Cash and Sonny. She whirled from partner to partner, having the time of her life. Everyone seemed genuinely happy for her and for Nate. And she was happy, too.

The only grim moment occurred when she danced with Barnaby Cotes.

"I wish you the best, Meggie," he told her stiffly. "But I can't say I believe you'll be happy with a man like that."

"Take a hike, Cotes," Nate muttered, cutting in on them before she had the chance to tell Barnaby that she could do without his condescending remarks.

Barnaby faded away into the crowd and Meggie found herself whirling in her husband's arms. She closed her eyes and smiled and wished the dance would never end.

"What did that creep say to you?" Nate asked in her ear.

"Nothing important."

"I never could stand him. He's a smug, self-righteous little—"

She put a hand over his mouth—her left hand, on which her wedding band gleamed. "Shh. Just dance."

He pulled her closer and didn't say another word.

They drove back to the Double-K together, long after dark, in the rental car that Nate planned to turn in on Monday. From then until they left for L.A., he would use the old GMC pickup from the Rising Sun to get around.

The nearly full moon seemed to light their way home. Meggie leaned her head on Nate's shoulder and watched it through the windshield, a silver disk with one side missing, in a night of a thousand stars. The moonlight spilled down on the rolling grasses, so they looked like sheets of liquid silver, rippling before the wind.

At last, Nate pulled into the yard. The lights were on in the bunkhouse. Sonny and Farrah had left the party to take the kids home over an hour before. Sonny's old hound dog, Scrapper, barked twice from the bunkhouse steps. And then he must have decided things were all right, because he didn't bark again.

Nate swung the car around and pulled up in front of the main house. He turned off the engine and the lights. They sat there, for a moment, with the wind sighing outside and the moonlight pouring down, silvering the yard.

Then Meggie lifted her head from Nate's shoulder. They shared a long glance.

And Nate said softly, "It shouldn't be in a bedroom."

She knew just what he meant. "Let's get going, then."

Half an hour later, Meggie rode out beside her husband, toward the Big Horns, black and craggy, like an absence of light against the night sky to the west. She rode Patriot, a fast little mare sired by her dear old Renegade. Nate had chosen a big black gelding that Meggie had named Indigo, since his coat shone almost purplish in the sun. Nate carried a rifle in his saddle scabbard, just to be on the safe side. And both of them had bedrolls tied on in back, with jackets wrapped inside.

They rode clear of the home place and then, as one, they reigned their horses in. For a moment, they just sat there, looking out over the land. Meggie leaned on the saddle horn, smiling into the wind, smelling sage and just a hint of pine from the mountains not far off. Somewhere an owl hooted. And a coyote let out one long, lonely howl.

They clucked their tongues softly at their horses and started out again. They didn't need words. They knew where they were going: to that spot by Crystal Creek where they had sat and talked for hours so many afternoons those first two years when they were almost children—and the best of friends. They rode overland, in and out of gates that took them back and forth from Rising Sun pastures to ones that belonged to the Double-K. They came up quiet and easy on the cattle in those pastures. As they went by, the long heads would lift. Wide-set bulging eyes, gleaming in the moonlight, would stare at them curiously. Then, in dismissal, the eyelids would flicker down—and the long heads would turn away.

At last they came to the dirt road that Nate had used at fourteen, when he went for a joyride in his grandpa's pickup. Meggie dug in her heels and Patriot took off, headed for the rise and the creek beyond. With a low laugh, Nate followed.

They raced over the ridge and down to the creek, laughing, the cool, clean wind in their faces, the moon showing the way. Over the years, successive spring thaws had changed the channel slightly. The old spot they used to favor no longer existed. They had to slow down and ride along above the bank, peering into the shadows of the willows and cottonwoods, looking for a likely place.

"Here," Nate said to her at last.

They unsaddled and hobbled their horses several yards from creek side. Then they hauled the saddles and bedrolls down to the grass near the water, where the trees and the lowness of the land made a break from the incessant, keening wind. Nate spread his sleeping bag on the grass; they would use Meggie's to put over them.

Finally they sat side by side on their makeshift marriage bed and pulled off their boots and their socks. Shyness found Meggie just as she started unbuttoning her shirt, making her heart beat too fast and all her fingers turn to thumbs. She sat still, licking her lips that had become as dry as late-summer grass, staring at the dark water rushing past not far away, thinking that she was absolutely terrified.

"Need some help?" Nate knelt before her.

A break in the tree cover overhead showed him to

her, silvered in moonlight. Unreality assailed her. Was this really happening?

It was. She knew it. He was her most precious, hopeless fantasy. And he was here with her tonight because she had sought him out and begged him to help her. And, in the end, he had come to her, unable to refuse her need. Her knight in shining armor, in spite of himself.

Wordless, she stared at him, at the shaggy jet hair, the chiseled face. His dark eyes, which so often watched the world in cold appraisal, were less cold now, maybe—but no less watchful.

To escape that gaze, she glanced down. He'd already taken off his shirt. She found herself staring at the hard muscles of his shoulders and arms, at the silky trail of black hair that curled out across his chest and then went down in a line over his hard belly, to disappear beneath the waistband of his worn jeans.

"Meggie?"

She made herself look into his eyes again. "I'm so scared all of a sudden...." The words came out sounding as weak as the cry of a sick calf, because her silly throat had clamped tight on her.

A rueful smile took one corner of that full Bravo mouth. "Meggie. You didn't go and *save* yourself, now, did you?"

Her face was flaming. She couldn't speak. She closed her eyes.

"Hell, Meggie," he whispered tenderly.

Not far away, one of the horses whickered softly. And the wind, beyond the shelter of the bank, whistled and moaned.

"Come on," he said. "Look at me."

She did, with great effort. And she tried to explain.

"I just, well, I didn't see any point, with anyone else, you know?" She laughed then, a pained sound, at herself more than anything. She remembered the girls he used to date, the wild ones, when he was so busy breaking her heart for the first time. "How could I ask you that? Of course you don't know."

"Meggie…"

She closed her eyes again, willed the hurts of the past away. Nate had never made any promises to her. He had always been honest. Brutally so. She had known she would never lie down with him. Because she wanted forever—and he wanted to be free.

Yet by some crazy miracle, here they were. On their wedding night. One moment in time that would never come again.

"Meggie."

She looked at him and gave him a smile that quivered only slightly at the corners. "Yes. I could use a little help," she said. "Somehow all my fingers have stopped working." She took his big hands, so warm and so strong, and put them on the top button of her shirt. "Please?"

His fingers moved, from one button to the next. The cool night air kissed her skin. He pulled the shirt out of her jeans, then took her wrists, one at a time, and undid the buttons there. His hands moved to her shoulders. And the shirt was gone.

Her bra was white lace; she'd worn it beneath the knee-length white dress she'd married him in. It had a front clasp. His fingers worked briefly there, pressing at the exact center of her chest. And the clasp came apart. He slid the bra off her shoulders and away, gently, considerately, reminding her of the way a child will do a task, with serious and complete concentration on every move.

He put his hands on her hips. "Stand up."

He steadied her as she rose. When she stood above him, he looked up the length of her body and she looked down at him, between the mounds of her own breasts, into the darkness of his eyes, a darkness she had longed for, always, all of her life, it seemed to her. She put her hands on her own belly, undid the top button of her fly. Then pulled. The zipper came open.

He hooked his hands in her waistband and took her jeans down, along with the white lace panties that matched her bra. She had to rest a hand on his shoulder for balance when she stepped clear of everything.

Swiftly, before she had time to ponder her own nakedness, he rose before her, and stripped down his own jeans. They faced each other at last, each totally nude. The wind blew, crying low. She shivered a little, still somewhat fearful—and poignantly aware that he was very much ready to make a baby with her.

He reached out a hand, ran it over the goose bumps on her arm. "More than damn *near* naked now."

She smiled, remembering that first day, when she had ridden up on Renegade without her jeans to find him beating out a fire with blanket.

"Cold?" he asked.

She rubbed her arms. "Yeah."

"Come on, then."

He guided her down to their bed on the grass, and pulled the cover over them. The sudden, cozy warmth was sheer heaven. He held her close, his body against hers, and he stroked her back—long, slow strokes. She understood his intention: that she become accustomed to his touch.

Meggie breathed slow and deep and let the sensations wash over her. She took in the scent of him. To her, he had always smelled like home, like breathing in the wind on the prairie: sage and dust and a hint of pine.

His body felt hot, hotter than her own, really. And big. And so strong, all sleek bone and ready muscle. The hair on his thighs scratched her a little. But it felt good. It felt right.

A few minutes before, he might have looked at her with tender pity, thinking her foolish to have *saved* herself. But right now, this moment, wrapped up tight with him, naked, she didn't feel foolish. She felt glad, right down to the deepest part of herself, that she would have the one man she wanted. That she had never settled for less.

He continued to stroke her, his hands moving over her neck, her shoulders and then between their bodies. He touched her breasts, tenderly, knowingly, bringing the nipples to hard, hungry peaks. His mouth followed his hands. When he took her nipple in his mouth, she threw her head back, moaning, as the sensation trailed its way down to her woman's core, which suddenly felt like a hot, moist flower, blooming, opening.

His hands were all over her. She lost track of each individual touch. The caresses were all one. He touched the blooming center of her, and she opened all the more for him.

Then he was rising above her, blocking out the dark trees, the night sky and the moon. He braced himself on his elbows. She knew he gazed down at her, serious and intent; though, with the moon behind him, she could not actually see his eyes. She felt him, at her tender entrance, as he positioned himself.

He thrust in, hard and clean. She let out one sharp, wounded cry.

And he lay still inside her, letting her body know him, giving her time to accept his invasion. He bent his head and found her mouth. The kiss they shared went on forever.

Three times, she thought. Three times, she had kissed this man. Once fourteen years ago, on the Fourth of July. Once just hours ago, so briefly, a light brushing of his lips on hers, to seal their wedding vows. And now. A third kiss. As they lay mated on the grass by Crystal Creek, beneath a cottonwood tree....

Down where he pressed into her, there was pain. And a fullness. Slowly, as he kissed her, the pain was fading. Becoming pleasure. And a hunger, to move. To seek a rhythm that would bring fulfillment shattering through them both.

With a long sigh, she adjusted herself, wrapping her legs around his. He simply kept kissing her, pausing only long enough to make a growling sound and to smile against her mouth.

She lifted her hips, taking him even more fully into her. Then she relaxed back into their grassy bed. He made that growling sound again.

And then he was moving. And she was moving with him. And their eternal kiss continued as their bodies moved together in an endless, rolling wave—like the grasses of the prairie, rippling on and on forever before the incessant wind.

Something rose within her, reaching. And she followed it, up and over the edge of the universe. Into a darkness that exploded with light. She held on to Nate, crying out. And he held on to her.

He whispered her name at the very end, as if it was

the only name that mattered, whispered it in agony and
joy, against her parted lips.

"Yes, Nate," she whispered back. "Yes." And
"Yes," again.

Chapter Five

Meggie woke at dawn to the sound of a meadowlark trilling out its high, piercing song. She looked over at Nate. Surprisingly, he slept on. And very peacefully, too, his cheek resting on his arm. Though she didn't want to wake him yet, she couldn't keep herself from staring at him just for a moment or two, knowing she wore a fool's grin on her face, and not giving a darn. Or course, Nate Bravo could never look soft, but he came pretty close to it, now in sleep. She thought of last night and her foolish grin widened.

Carefully, Meggie slid from under the covers and pulled on her clothes, including the jacket she'd left flung over her saddle, ready to pull on against the morning chill. Patriot, not far away, saw her moving about and snorted at her in question. She shot the horse a look and the mare snorted once more, then bent her head to nip delicately at what was left of the grass around her hooves.

Nate stirred a little, as Meggie was pulling on her boots. She sat very still, watching him, but he didn't open his eyes. Quietly, Meggie rose and tiptoed away. Once she was far enough from Nate that she didn't think the sound of her boots brushing the grass would wake him, she picked up her pace. She walked briskly, up the rise they'd come down the night before. At the top, she sat facing the creek.

From her perch, she could see the horses, nibbling the stubs of grass they'd already chewed down during the night. She could also see Nate, under the blankets by the side of the creek. And if she raised her eyes, she could see the Big Horns. Very soon, the sun would break over the horizon behind her and flood the craggy peaks with morning light.

She reached in the pocket of her jacket and found the envelope she'd stuck in there the night before. It contained a letter from her father, which G. Vernon Bannister had given her on the same day he informed her of the contents of her father's will.

Meggie opened the letter carefully and smoothed it on her knee. She had read it before, of course. A hundred times, at least—during those first awful days after she'd learned what Jason Kane had done to her. She had read it in rage and hurt and a faint hope that someday, somehow, she would let herself forgive him.

She read it now as the sun hit the Big Horns and the day truly began:

My dearest Megan,
I know how you must be feeling right now. And I got to admit, I'm glad I don't have to face you.

But something had to be done. And I have done it. And that's that.

I've told you more than one time how I fear for you, fear that you've put all of your love into the land. And how I worry it's not healthy. That if you're not careful, you'll end up like me, with no one beside you in the darkest part of the night. In plain speaking, Meggie girl, you could end up worse than me, because at least your mother gave me you before she took off. But the way you're headed, you won't even have a child to give the land to when you go.

It pleases me that your cousin has brought his family to the Double-K. I hope they stay on. But a cousin is not a husband. And those two children of Sonny's are not your own. I want you to have children of your own.

And don't go thinking I don't know my own part in what's happened to you. Your mother was the only woman I ever loved. And if I couldn't have her, I didn't want anyone else. I waited and waited for her to come back to us, though she told me when she left that she was never coming back. Still, even after I got word of her death, some crazy part of me kept hoping to see her again. I'm still hoping, to tell you true. And I know I passed that narrow way of loving on to you.

You never talked about Nathan Bravo to me. But I know that he was the one. And I don't know whether you told him and he turned you down— or he just plain never asked. But he is gone from you now, living far away. And all you've allowed yourself is the Double-K. It's not enough.

Anyways, I guess you know I have been sick

for a while. And the closer my time came, the more it got clear to me just what I needed to do.

By now, Mr. Bannister has told you the terms of my will. And I know you're probably mad as a peeled rattler at your old man. But I sincerely hope, over time, that you will come to understand why I've done what I've done. To understand, and maybe even to forgive. Hell, if you find happiness because of this, you might even thank me one day. And in any case, if my plan doesn't work out, the sale of the herd and the home place should give you enough of a stake to start again.

Megan May, when I look back on my life, I see your eyes. It feels to me that *you* are why I lived at all. And what I want for you is a shot at a marriage. A damn long shot, I know. But a chance, anyway. And at least one child. Someone to be the reason why *you* lived, when you're old and used up and waiting for death to ease the pain that eats you from inside.

I do love you, Meggie. And I did this for you.

                              Your father, Jason Levi Kane

Carefully, Meggie folded the letter and put it back in the envelope. She put the envelope in her pocket. Right then, from somewhere behind her, another meadowlark burst into song. She stared at the Big Horns, now bathed in sunlight. And she thought of her father.

Jason Kane *had* loved Mia Stephens Kane with all of his heart. He had met her on a trip to Denver, and brought her home to share his life. She stayed long enough to have their baby. And then she left. Meggie had no memories of her at all. Still, Meggie's childhood had felt complete—because of Jason Kane.

The sun on the mountains shone so bright it made her squint. She drew up her legs, wrapped her arms around them and rested her cheek on her knees.

Her father might not have intended for her to go after troublesome Nate Bravo in order to fulfill the terms of his will. But she *had* gone after Nate. And for a time, she would have him. Thus, in a way, her father had forced her to go out and pursue her heart's desire.

Of course, it wouldn't last....

Meggie closed her eyes and smiled to herself. What ever really lasted anyway? God willing, she'd have a few shining, wonderful months with the man who owned her heart—and she'd have his baby. It was much more than she had ever dared to hope for in all the lonely years since he had turned her love away.

Keeping her eyes shut, Meggie lifted her head and tipped her face to the wind. Right then and there, she made a promise to herself. She vowed that she would not try to hold Nate when it ended. She'd take these few precious months to treasure and she would set him free with a smile when the time came. Moreover, while they were together, she would not cling to him, or pressure him with talk of love.

Just as the vow was made, she heard Nate's footsteps, whispering through the grass. The footsteps stopped a few feet from her. She opened her eyes and looked at him.

"You okay?" he asked.

She nodded. He hadn't bothered to pull on his shirt and his muscular chest was pebbled with goose bumps in the cold morning air. Also, his hair stuck out at all angles and he had a red sleep mark on his cheek where he'd lain on his arm. She thought he was the most gorgeous sight she'd ever beheld.

He faked a mean frown. "What are you staring at?"

"You." Suddenly suspicious, she narrowed her eyes at him. "How long have you been awake?"

He grinned. "Since you slid out from under the covers. But you seemed like a woman on a mission, the way you pulled on your clothes so carefully and then crept away. I figured you wanted a little time alone."

She would have shown him the letter then if it hadn't included mention of him and how much she loved him. References to her undying love could be read as putting pressure on him, which she had just silently sworn not to do.

"Well?" he asked.

"Well what?"

He dropped down beside her. "*Did* you want a little time alone?"

She leaned his way, still clutching her drawn-up knees, so their bodies touched. "I did. Thanks."

He looked in her eyes and something lovely and intimate passed between them. "No problem."

She dared to wrap her arm around his shoulder. His skin felt wonderful under her hand, so smooth and tight, the muscles beneath as hard as stones, but more resilient. "Aren't you cold?"

He shrugged and looked out toward the sun-bright mountains. "It's not bad."

Behind them, the meadowlark sang some more. Along the crest of the rise, about fifty feet away, a jackrabbit rose up on its hind legs, sniffed the air and then turned to hop off, long ears twitching. Somebody's stomach growled, but they were sitting so close Meggie couldn't tell whose.

She chuckled. "We should get back to the house. Get some breakfast. And some oats for the poor horses."

He looked at her again. "No."

His curtness startled her a little. "What?"

He turned toward her slightly and slid his hand between the open sides of her down jacket. She sucked in a quick, surprised breath as he began unbuttoning her shirt.

"I've always wanted you," he said conversationally, "since we were kids." His fingers had made swift work of the buttons. Now she felt his hand sliding under the cup of her bra. His hand was cold. She shivered a little. He made a low, soothing sound as he cradled her breast.

He spoke in that casual tone again. "I wanted to do all kinds of things to your body. And you knew it." He toyed with her nipple. "You were furious at me, because I wouldn't give in and come after you. Weren't you?"

Meggie said nothing. She felt pretty much pole-axed—but in a delicious sort of way. The moment he touched her, her body came alive. Every sensation became acute. Arousal spread through her, pooling in her belly, making everything loose and ready. Even the slight soreness caused by the night before had a need to it, as if it hungered to be made sorer still.

"Weren't you mad at me, Meggie May?" He unclasped her bra.

She melted. Opened. Bloomed.

"Meggie. Answer."

She forced herself to reply. "Yes. I was mad at you."

He smoothed the sides of her bra out of his way. "But I didn't touch you, except that one kiss, on the Fourth of July. I knew the price of touching you—marriage. Turn toward me." She did as he commanded. He took her hips and pulled her to him, lifting her so she straddled his lap, there on that rise, with the wind and the dewy grass moving all around them.

She could feel him, through her jeans, as hard and ready as she was meltingly willing. He smiled, a slow, devastatingly sexy smile. "But now. Hell. I've paid the price. I've married you. And for the next few months, it's kind of my job. To want you. Right?"

She drew in a long, shaky breath. "Right."

He slid both hands inside her coat and tugged on her shirt, until it was out of her Wranglers. Then he gathered her close, his hands splayed on her bare back. "Before breakfast is always a good time," he whispered in her ear.

She quivered, and pressed herself closer to him, her breasts against his broad, hard chest.

He instructed, "Say, 'Yes, Nate.'"

Obediently, she parroted, "Yes, Nate."

"Wrap your legs around me. I'll take you back to the blankets."

She hooked her boots around his waist. He got his feet beneath him and rocked back on his heels. With a low grunt, he stood. And then he started down the rise to where the blankets waited.

In the golden days that followed, Nate worked right alongside Megan and Sonny. As it turned out, they needed the extra pair of hands, because Lev found a better-paying job and left them a few days after the wedding. The day Lev took off, Meggie told Nate that she would just go ahead and pay him Lev's wages.

Nate laughed. "Forget it, Meggie May. I'm not taking your money."

"But if you're going to work, it only seems fair that you—"

"Quiet. I don't want to hear it."

"But it's not right."

"Look at it this way. I'm working for something that will someday belong to my kid, right?"

"If everything goes the way we hope."

"So consider it child support."

"But—"

He only shook his head. "Say thank-you."

She did.

"And give me a kiss."

She did that, too.

Nate fit right in. He knew the work—better than Lev had, certainly. After all, Nate was Ross Bravo's grandson and had helped out at the Rising Sun from the age of fourteen on. He could string a fence with the best of them.

And he never shirked in the endless, backbreaking work of clearing the ditches so that precious water would find its way to the cattle and the alfalfa fields. Sometimes they dug the ditches out; sometimes they burned out the swamp grass that choked them. And sometimes, when they burned, the fires got away from them, creeping along underneath the thick grasses to pop up here and there, taunting them with how easily a prairie fire can get a hold.

When they cut hay that summer, Nate usually drove the swather. The swather was designed to both cut and windrow the hay, leaving it laid out in a neat row, ready for the baler, which they wouldn't bring round until the hay had a chance to cure in the hot summer sun.

Once, when they were cutting alfalfa, Meggie climbed onto the small platform near where Nate sat to drive. She held on tight while he went up and down the field, with the big blades turning, throwing the hay up into a pair of canvas rollers that spit it out in a long row behind. She laughed, over the noise of the engine, enjoying herself immensely, in spite of the bits of grass and dirt blown in her face by the wind. Life never got much better than this, to be here with Nate, essentially living out her dearest fantasy—of the two of them, married and working together every day.

Nate yelled, "Pay attention—hang on." She glanced back at the big sharp blades and took his advice to heart.

When the field was cut, that wonderful smell perfumed the air. There was nothing like the scent of cut alfalfa. Sweet and grassy, with a hint of spice from the little purple flowers it produced. Cut alfalfa was the smell of summer, pure and simple, to Meggie's mind.

Beyond haying and fencing and burning ditches, there were always weeds to poison. Especially sage and leafy spurge. Sage had been the bane of the prairie for generations. But spurge had been brought over from Europe more recently by some botanist who didn't know the kind of trouble he would end up causing.

Leafy spurge was a pretty green plant with tiny yellow flowers. Its roots went deep and it grew in dense clumps, forcing out the native grass wherever it took hold. And in the western United States, it seemed to be taking hold with a vengeance. Cattle wouldn't eat it; even most of the wildlife left it alone. And it was hard to kill, even with powerful herbicides. So, for local ranchers, poisoning spurge had become a summer-long activity. They treated it with Tordon, a chemical weed killer that came in both liquid and pellet form.

Most often that summer, when they poisoned leafy spurge on the Double-K, Nate drove the pickup, since he was so adept at getting a vehicle in and out of the kind of places Meggie wouldn't have even imagined it could go. As Nate drove, either Meggie or Sonny would work from the bed of the pickup, spraying like crazy or scattering pellets.

And of course, there was the constant work of checking the cattle, bringing in the ones with foot rot or cancer eye for treatment, keeping an eye on their watering holes to make sure they still had water and that no animal had gotten itself bogged down in the mud. And moving them, making choices about the culls—cattle they planned to sell off—so they would be ready for shipping day in the fall.

Then, at night, the big, old bed in the master bedroom was waiting for them. They worked hard there, as well, to make the baby that Meggie needed so much. Neither of them minded that particular job in the least.

Naturally, Nate insisted on bull riding in the August rodeo in Buffalo. Meggie's heart stopped beating for the entire seven seconds he stayed on. The bull he drew was a mean one, and he barely avoided getting stomped. When it was over, he told Meggie he was getting too damn old for such foolishness. She knew him well enough to disagree with him.

She said, "You love it and you know it. And you'll be riding bulls when you're sixty if you don't break your neck first."

He put his arm around her and bussed her on the cheek. "Hell. You got me nailed."

He smelled of manure. She looked up at his dirty face and wondered how it was possible for her heart to hold so much joy without bursting apart.

Once in August and once at the beginning of September, Nate returned to L.A.—the first time to testify in a trial and later to do a little sleuthing for some software firm that had sent a lot of business his way. But he never stayed away for more than a week. Meggie was happy, living in the now. She strictly honored her secret vow; not once did she speak of love or permanence. And Nate seemed as content as Meggie had ever seen him. She couldn't help priding herself on how well things were going between them.

But neither Meggie's happiness nor Nate's apparent contentment could stop the seasons from changing. Jealously, Meggie noted the signs of autumn's approach. The blackbirds gathered in the fields, getting ready for the long trip south. And the geese could be seen flying in their vee formations through the cloudy sky. The cottonwoods along Crystal Creek started to turn. And mornings brought frost that blackened the leaves of Farrah's pumpkin vines.

Meggie and Sonny discussed the different offers that had been made on the steers they were planning to sell.

They were still holding out, at that point, for a better price.

One September morning, Meggie and Nate decided they'd take the GMC pickup out to what they called the Ridge Pasture, a couple of miles from the house. They had loaded the back of the pickup with half barrels full of a molasses-based vitamin-and-mineral supplement, which they fed to the cattle to round out their diet.

Meggie pointed to the black clouds rolling in over Cloud Peak. "Storm coming," she said. She was smiling. She loved a storm, loved the charged smell in the air as the storm clouds gathered.

"We can beat it," Nate said.

They took off at Nate's usual breakneck pace, along the dirt roads made by mining companies and oil speculators that crisscrossed the ranch. In the Ridge Pasture, the empty tubs were ranged along the crest of the high ridge after which the pasture had been named, away from any water source. To get to the sweet, sticky mixture, the cattle had to move around, rather than sticking by their favorite holes, eating the grass down to nothing in one spot. Nate shifted the pickup into low and it groaned its way up the dirt road to the crest.

At ridgetop, under a heavy, threatening sky, they jumped out and began switching the full barrels for the empty ones, which they tossed into the back of the pickup. Lightning forked down on a neighboring ridge just as the last empty barrel hit the pickup bed. The air smelled of ozone. Thunder reverberated across the dry, waiting land.

All at once, the wind grew fierce. The soot-black clouds piled overhead began to drop their rain. Meggie tipped up her face and opened her mouth. The wetness tasted wonderful. She giggled to herself.

She could almost hear her father's voice. "Meggie May, you're a durn fool. You want to make yourself a human lightning rod?"

So all right. She was a durn fool. And it felt terrific. Lightning flashed again and thunder struck out and rolled, booming, off toward the mountains. The rain came thick and fast, big, cold, sloppy drops, blown hard against her by the whipping wind.

Down by the creek in the lower part of the pasture, everything had become shrouded in mist.

The rain turned to hail just as Nate grabbed her hand. "Come on!"

She went with him, into the cab of the truck.

The hail pelted the roof, pinging and snapping. Unlike Meggie, who was having a ball, Nate had his mind on getting the hell back to the house before the roads turned to gumbo. He reached for the key he'd left stuck in the ignition.

And Meggie put her hand on his arm. She laughed. God, he did love her laugh....

"Nate. Wait. Listen."

He looked at her. Water dripped off the brim of her hat and onto the seat between them. She was soaked through. And so was he.

"We should get the hell back to the house," he grumbled.

"It's all right. The lightning can't hurt us now that we're in the truck."

"What about the roads, Meggie?"

She wrinkled her nose, because she had no answer to

that one. Finally, she simply shrugged. "Forget the roads."

"Meggie..."

"Shh."

"Meggie."

"You're not listening."

"Listening to what?"

She pointed at the roof of the cab, her head cocked, one eyebrow lifted. "Hear that?"

"Right. Hail. What a surprise."

"No. Imagine we're popcorn. Popping."

He glared at her for a moment more, and then couldn't keep it up. The hail beating down on the pickup did sound a little like corn exploding in a hot pan.

She slid across the seat and right up against him. "Nate." She took off his hat and dropped it on the dashboard. And then she did the same with her own. She nuzzled his neck.

"What are you up to?" he asked, though he had a pretty good idea. And so did his body. Already his jeans had become too snug.

"Nate," was all she said. She put her hand on his cheek and guided his mouth around. And then her lips touched his, cool at first, from the rain and the wind. But not cool for long...

With a groan, Nate gave himself to the kiss.

He loved the taste of her, so clean and sweet. And the smell of her, that woodsy scent with something flowery in it, just a little bit musky now, from tossing the mineral tubs around.

Outside, the hail had turned to rain again. The two in the cab didn't notice.

Nate pulled Meggie's thermal shirt out of her jeans and undid her bra. But he didn't take anything off, just in case someone happened to come along.

With a low laugh, she leaned back against the passenger door and stuck out a boot. "Pull."

Nate pulled—one wet boot and then the other. He helped her shimmy out of her jeans and her white cotton panties, too. Then he slid over to join her on the passenger side of the seat, so the steering wheel wouldn't interfere.

The windows had fogged over completely by the time she unzipped him and got his own clothes out of the way enough that she could mount him. He slid into her heat and softness, groaning with the sweet agony of it.

"Nate, Nate, Nate…" She whispered his name against his lips as she rode him in slow, long, deep strokes. Now and then, she would pause, with him halfway out of her. He would stand it for as long as he could. And then, with a moan, he would take her hips and pull her down onto him again.

Outside, the hard rain slowed to a steady downpour. To Nate, the drumming sound of it against the roof and hood of the pickup was mesmerizing. Erotic.

Meggie moaned and kissed him. Her body moved on his. He didn't know what it was about her. Somehow, she made it all stronger, fiercer, more complete—and more plain fun—than any sex he'd ever had. She fit him just right, as maybe he'd always known that she would. She knew how to laugh. And how to play. When to tease. And when to give him what he wanted without any frills.

He let his head drop back as completion rolled over him, mowing him down like a waiting hay field under the blades of a relentless swather. He pushed himself high and hard into her. She whimpered—and pushed right back. He felt her going over with him, her body expanding and contracting around him. He reached out, blindly, and pulled her close against him, rucking up her shirt and bra so that he could feel her bare skin.

For several minutes, they just sat there, all wrapped up together in the steamy cab, as the rain droned on outside.

Finally, he muttered, "We're in for it now, trying to get out of here."

She had her hands under his shirt and was idly stroking him. "We'll manage."

He returned the favor, running his hands back and forth along the smooth length of her bare thighs. She sighed a little and nuzzled closer. Nate went on caressing her, thinking that he almost wished they would never make that baby, that they could just go on working at it indefinitely.

And boy, had they been working at it. Once or twice a night, since the wedding. And sometimes in the daytime, like now. Any time the slightest opportunity presented itself. If that doctor in Billings had been right about them, she should be pregnant already.

He frowned, his hand going still on her thigh as he realized that, to his knowledge, she hadn't had a period since he had started sleeping in her bed. But then he relaxed again, as he remembered those days he had been gone. The two trips had been just about a month apart.

With a long sigh, he rolled his head toward the driver's side of the cab. Through the fog on the window, he saw something move.

"Meggie," he whispered low.

"Um?"

He signaled with his head. She looked over.

Meggie gasped. "Oh, dear Lord..."

And then Nate reached out and brushed a hand over the foggy glass. As the glass cleared, they found themselves staring into the wide, solemn eyes of a Hereford steer.

Meggie leaned across the seat. "You are *steak*," she said to the long, white face on the other side of the window.

The steer turned his head and let out an extended, thoroughly insolent, "Mooo!"

Fall work began.

They gathered the cattle they planned to drive to the feedlots for sale. Gathering days were long ones, spent mostly in the saddle, herding and moving the culls into separate pastures from the breeding stock and the calves.

Soon after fall gathering came shipping day, when they drove the cattle to the feedlots, where the vet and the brand inspector checked them over and then Meggie collected her money from the buyers waiting there.

In the last weeks of October, they began weaning the calves. Weaning allowed the cows a little time to build up their nutritional stores, before the calves that were growing inside them started draining off their once again.

By then, the long Wyoming winter had begun to close in. Meggie, Nate and Sonny gathered and moved the calves with the wind in their faces and sleet stinging their cheeks. During weaning, they also took the time to put the calves in the chute and pour Spot-On over their backs, a topical medication for the control of grubs. They had the vet over to vaccinate the heifers against certain contagious diseases. In the end, weaning amounted to a lot of messy work in bad weather.

But they got through it. By the first week of November, that year's calves were on their own.

And Nate wanted to return to L.A.

Meggie knew it was time to go. But she didn't even want to think about leaving. She wanted to go on as they had been. She longed to enjoy with Nate the relatively quiet time that was coming up, to spend the holidays together with him here, at home.

She knew she had no right to want those things. She had vowed not to cling or try to hold him. And stalling about leaving brought her perilously close to breaking her vow.

But she didn't care. She cheated on her vow and stalled. Twice, when he reminded her that they had to make plans to leave, she pretended not to hear him. The third time he brought the subject up, they were in bed. Since she was lying right on top of him, kissing him, it was pretty difficult to fake inattention. So she suddenly found she had to go to the bathroom. She slid out of the bed.

"Meggie, what the hell—" Nate demanded.

"I'll be back in a flash."

"Meggie..."

She flew across the room and disappeared into the bathroom before he could say any more. She stayed in there for a very long time. And when she came out, he'd turned off the bedside lamp.

"Nate?" she asked nervously into the darkness.

"Come to bed, Meggie," he answered, sounding resigned. "Go to sleep."

But Meggie knew that Nate wasn't the kind of man a woman could stall for long. And she was right. After dinner on the second Saturday in November, she went up to the room they shared and found him packing. He zipped up the big duffel bag he used for a suitcase and carried it with finality over to the door where she stood watching him.

He dropped the bag at her feet. "I'm leaving in the morning."

She looked down at the bag and then up at him, her love for him washing over her like a powerful wave, cutting off her air. She wanted to grab him. And hold him. And never let him go.

"Cash will fly me to Denver," he said. Cash had his own plane. "And from there, I've got a direct flight to LAX."

His hair had gotten hung up on the collar of his shirt. She reached out and freed it, then stroked it smooth.

He caught her hand. "Are you coming with me?"

She closed her eyes, swallowed and then made herself drag in a breath and speak. "I'll...be along."

He looked at her piercingly. And then he dropped her hand. "I know you don't want to leave. I know how you are, about this ranch. About your life here. But I have to go, Meggie. I have a damn life, too, you know.''

"I know."

"I can't keep turning down jobs. Word gets out I'm unavailable. It cuts into the offers I get."

She thought of the money she'd wanted him to take. It would have helped to make up for the business he'd lost. But she wasn't going to bring up the money. He'd made himself more than clear on that issue. "I understand."

"We agreed—"

She reached out, put her fingers over his lips. "Shh. I know. I just…need a little time. Is that okay?"

"Hell." He grabbed her wrist. And then his lips were moving against her fingers, kissing them.

"Oh, Nate…"

He tugged. She went into his arms. His mouth came down on hers, hot and demanding, full of fire and need.

He kicked the door closed, scooped her up and carried her over to the bed.

Nate woke well before dawn. He turned his head and looked at Meggie. She slept on her side, facing him, a slight frown marring her brow. He wanted to reach out and stroke that frown away. But he knew if he woke her, she'd only try to keep him from going.

And not with words. Meggie May Kane was too honorable a woman to argue against something she'd already agreed to. No, she would work to hold him with looks. And with touches. With soft sighs. With the formidable power her sweet body had over his.

But Nate Bravo did not intend to be held—no matter

how tempting the looks, the sighs and the caresses. He'd never lied to her about that. He was doing what he could for her. If she wanted to keep her ranch, she would just have to come to L.A. as she had agreed to do.

The frown lines faded as he watched her face. Her wide mouth turned up in a dreamy smile. She made a small, contented sound and snuggled lower into the nest of blankets.

All he wanted at that moment was to touch her. To put his hands and his mouth on her. To pull back the blankets and—

He had to get the hell out. Now.

Quietly, he turned toward his side of the bed and slid carefully out from under the covers. The room was icy. But he didn't mind the cold. It got his blood pumping faster, made him want to hurry. He pulled on his clothes—all but his boots—mindful not to make the slightest sound. Finally, he took an envelope from a side pocket of his bag. Just as he was propping it against the alarm clock on the nightstand, Meggie rolled toward him with a sigh. He froze.

But she didn't wake. She slept on. And he stood there like the fool he'd somehow allowed himself to become for her, watching. Wanting…

Nate closed his eyes. He sucked in a slow breath. And then he turned, scooped up his bag and walked out the door.

Meggie opened her eyes at the sound of the front door closing downstairs. Instantly wide-awake, she looked over her shoulder to where Nate should be sleeping. He wasn't there.

With a small, frantic cry, she threw off the covers, scooped up her nightgown from the end of the bed and yanked it over her nakedness. She heard a car door creak open outside, so she flew to the window. Below, in the yard, melting patches of dirty white spotted the dark, bare ground, the remains of the first real snowfall a few days before. She watched Nate toss his bag into the pickup and then climb in after it.

Meggie shivered. The floor felt like a slab of ice under her bare feet; the fire she always left burning in the old black heat stove downstairs must have gone completely out. Rooted to the spot in spite of the cold, she wrapped her arms around herself and stared out the window as the reluctant engine of the pickup sputtered to life. She went on watching as Nate drove down the drive, past the bunkhouse and the barn, the corrals and the outbuildings, toward the gate that led to the road. She didn't move from the window until he turned onto the road and she could no longer see his taillights through the thick darkness of the cloudy, moonless night.

Her gaze fell on the envelope propped on the nightstand. She grabbed it and dropped to the edge of the bed, scooping up her heavy shawl from the bedpost and wrapping it around herself. As she tore into the envelope, her toes found their way into her warm sheepskin slippers, which she always kept waiting by the side of the bed.

Inside the envelope she found a business card and a key. She reached out and flipped on the lamp. The card read *Bravo Investigative Services* at the top, then on the second line: DOMESTIC * CIVIL * CRIMINAL. Be-

low that, with asterisks between, was a list of the kinds
of services he performed: Background Checks * Missing Persons * Child Custody * Skip Tracing * Premar-
ital * Divorce * Process Serving. At the bottom was the
phone number she'd found in the L.A. phone book four
months before, and what appeared to be the number of
his private investigator's license.

Meggie turned the card over. On the back Nate had
scrawled an address, an apartment number and another
phone number—presumably, his private phone. His
message was clear: she had his address and the key to
his apartment. The rest was up to her.

Up to her…

Meggie's stomach clenched. And then she felt everything in it start to rise.

Tossing the card and the key on the nightstand, she
ran for the bathroom.

Chapter Six

The porcelain commode was so cold Meggie's hands ached when she touched it, but still she was grateful to have made it in time. When the heaving finally stopped, she sat in a heap for long minutes, bent over the bowl, waiting, just in case it wasn't over. Finally, when nothing more came up, she slumped against the tub beside her, breathing slowly and carefully, feeling weak, lost and lonely.

And more than a little bit guilty.

She had not had a period since before her wedding night. And she had been sure, for weeks now, that she was carrying Nate's baby.

Strange, she thought bleakly, as she clutched her shawl closer around her, how easy it had been to maintain the lie. At first, she had told herself that she couldn't be absolutely certain. What did a missed period or two mean, after all?

Since she was normally as regular as clockwork, a missed period meant a lot. But she'd just put that idea right out of her mind. And later, when she could no longer deny the truth to herself, she simply didn't allow herself to think about it.

Surprisingly, Nate had helped her. He had never once asked about those periods she didn't have. More than likely, he'd trusted her honesty, believed that she'd tell him if all of their lovemaking had produced its intended result. And nature had colluded with her as well; the rare times, like just now, when morning sickness had overwhelmed her, Nate hadn't been nearby.

Shame sent a flush up her neck, pushing back the cold a little. Nate had a living to make, after all. She had kept him from it needlessly—and even told herself it was his own fault if he lost money, since he'd turned down the sizable amount she'd offered him to make up for whatever business he lost.

Groaning a little, she dragged herself to her feet and turned on the bathroom light. Her face, in the mirror over the sink, looked pale and sunken eyed. She splashed freezing water on her cheeks and brushed her teeth.

Then she wandered back into the bedroom. It was after four. She might as well get dressed, get the fire going downstairs and get a head start on the day.

But instead of pulling on her clothes, she dropped to the edge of the bed again. She picked up the key Nate had left her and looked down at it in her open palm. She had to tell him. He should have been told weeks ago.

And he would be told. Immediately. She would give him time to make his way home, and then she would call him and say that their goal had been reached; she'd be sending him his divorce papers as soon as the baby was born.

Her fingers closed around the key.

Then again, to call him would be cowardly. The least she could do would be to tell him about the baby face-to-face....

Two days later, on Monday, Meggie got off a plane at LAX. A cabdriver in a black pin-striped suit with a pink turban wrapped around his head took her to Nate's apartment in West Hollywood. Meggie spent the long drive staring out the window of the cab at palm trees, a cloudless sky and streets clogged with cars. She felt a little dazed. When she had boarded the small commuter plane in Sheridan, it had been fifteen degrees outside, with snow in the forecast. She'd been bundled into her heaviest coat, grateful for its warmth. In Denver, where she'd caught a commercial flight, it had been cold and gray and well below freezing. Here, the sun shone down, the temperature had to be in the seventies—and her heavy coat was just something unnecessary to lug around.

Finally, the driver pulled up in front of a two-story Spanish-style building with rough white walls and a red tile roof. "Here we go, yes," he said in a pleasant, rather singsongy voice. White teeth flashed in his brown face. "Your place to which you are visiting." He pointed cheerfully at the meter and sang out the exorbitant cost of the ride.

Without so much as a gasp of dismay, Meggie paid him, adding on a generous tip. She smiled to herself, thinking that she was really getting cosmopolitan. This was her third cab ride—the other two having occurred during her brief visit last July. Already she could pay a cabbie without flinching.

Apparently pleased with her and the tip she'd given him, the cabbie jumped out, took her small suitcase from the trunk and opened the car door for her. He held out his hand. "Allow me, yes?"

She gave him her hand and he helped her to the sidewalk.

"You have a real good time, now, okay?" His turban bobbed up and down as he nodded.

She promised that she would, and then found herself standing there on the sidewalk, with her coat over her arm, waving as he got back in his cab and drove away. Once he disappeared around the corner, she shook herself, picked up her suitcase and squared her shoulders. Her head high and her step determined, she marched up the walk to Nate's building.

She walked up one side of the building, discovered she'd gone the wrong way and retraced her steps, trying the other side next. By the time she found Nate's apartment, in the back, upstairs, she'd seen the dimensions of the place. It was small, with six apartments, three up and three down, each with an outside entrance.

By the time she stood before Nate's door, Meggie's heart was beating way too fast and sweat had broken out on her upper lip. Determined to face him and get it over with, she set down her suitcase and lifted the iron knocker. She gave three good raps. And then she waited.

Nothing happened.

She knocked again. Still no answer.

At that point, Meggie's heart had stopped trying to beat its way out of her chest. It looked as if Nate had gone out—which meant a possible reprieve. Coward that she was, she suddenly felt much better about everything. If she could just go inside and sit down for a few moments, collect herself and relax a little, she felt certain she'd be much more ready to tell Nate about his upcoming fatherhood the minute he walked in the door.

Meggie dug the key out of her purse and unlocked the door. Just in case he might be there after all, she stuck her head in first and called, "Nate? Are you here?"

As expected, she got no answer. There was a mail slot in the door. And the floor beyond the threshold was strewn with envelopes.

Feeling like an intruder, Meggie stepped inside and set her suitcase and purse on the floor, draping her coat over them. Then she closed the door. Nate had three locks: one on the door handle, the dead bolt she'd unlocked to get in and a heavy chain. Remembering that this was L.A., Meggie engaged them all.

By then, she was tired of trying to step around Nate's mail. So she bent and scooped it up, after which she rose again and leaned against the door, getting her bearings.

She stood in a long hallway that extended to the left and right from the door. To the right, she could see that the hallway opened up to a living area.

She went left, where she found what she needed: a bathroom—and a very attractive one, too. It had built-in cabinets, a big, deep tub, plush wine-colored towels and black and white tile. She set the mail on the sink counter and made use of the toilet. Once she was through, she washed her hands and gathered up the mail again. She peeked into the other two rooms at that end of the hall. One contained a huge bed on a wrought-iron frame with a fabulous silk comforter of a deep-

maroon color. There were black-lacquer bureaus and
beautiful lamps with black wire-mesh bases and raw-
silk shades in maroon and midnight blue. The other
room contained a beat up old desk, a file cabinet, a
computer, a phone, an answering machine and a fax
machine.

Down the hall the other way, not far beyond the front
door, Meggie discovered a small kitchen. The kitchen
was tiled like the bathroom, in black and white. A
sturdy oak table stood beneath a big window at the far
end. On the table, sat a blue ceramic pitcher. Out of the
pitcher bloomed a bouquet of yellow lilies.

An envelope waited, propped against the pitcher,
bearing her name in Nate's bold hand. Meggie set
Nate's mail on the table and reached for the envelope.
She opened it slowly, not sure she wanted to know what
was inside.

She found a note, two keys and three one hundred–
dollar bills. The note read:

I've taken a job and should return by Wednesday
or Thursday, the thirteenth or fourteenth. I figure
you'll need transportation. The keys are to the blue
Volvo in the carport in back. It should get you
wherever you need to go. The money's in case
you're short of cash. For anything else you need
to know, ask Dolores Garnica, who owns and man-
ages the place. She's downstairs in the front apartment.

Still carrying the note, Meggie wandered into the living room and dropped into a big, jewel-green easy chair.
She stared down at the note: Wednesday or Thursday.

That would be two or three days. She'd wanted a reprieve—but not that much of one.

Feeling slightly stunned, Meggie slumped back in the chair and looked around the high-ceilinged room. A few feet away, two sapphire-blue couches faced each other, a low glass table between them. The bare hardwood floor gleamed in the spill of light from the tall, six-over-six windows on two walls. There was even a leafy, healthy-looking palm in one corner. The teak bookcases held lots of books—as well as an extensive collection of crystals, geodes and shells. Meggie found the room spare and dramatic. And quite beautiful.

It surprised her. So did the rest of the apartment— except for Nate's office. That room, so Spartan and utilitarian, with its scarred desk and green roll-up blinds, seemed more like Nate's kind of place.

Meggie smiled to herself. It came to her that she'd always thought of Nate as living in a kind of exile. The way she saw it, Nate had been born to be hers. Born to work the Double-K beside her, just as they'd been doing for the past few perfect months. Meggie had learned to live with the fact that Nate refused to surrender to his fate with her. But she'd always been certain he must be living a mean and barren life. Instead, she found lots of windows and intense colors, hardwood floors and seashells. And yellow lilies in a pitcher on the kitchen table.

Tired from the long trip, reprieved for a while whether she liked it or not, Meggie leaned back in the big, soft chair and closed her eyes.

When she woke, the room was dark and someone was knocking on the door. Yawning, Meggie pulled herself from the chair, flicked on a lamp and went to answer. She looked through the peephole before opening the door. On the other side she saw a pleasant-faced older woman with gray wings in her black hair. She wore a flowered housedress over her plump, full-bosomed figure.

Meggie disengaged all the locks and pulled open the door.

"You are Megan Bravo." The woman smiled, a smile that made her pleasant face beautiful. "I hope."

"Yes. I'm Megan."

"And I am Dolores." She stuck out a hand, which Meggie shook. Her grip was warm and firm. "This building is mine," she said with great pride. "And so is the one next door. Mr. Bravo said to watch for you. It is something very special when Mr. Bravo asks a favor."

"Yes. I guess you're right."

"So I want to show him, since he is a good tenant, that I do not take this honor lightly. I have been gone all day, but Benny, my husband, who owns these buildings with me, said he saw you go by our door in the afternoon with your little suitcase." She cast a quick glance down at the suitcase in question, which still waited near the door with Meggie's coat and purse. "Hmm. That is a *very* small suitcase for a bride to bring to her new home."

"I'm, um, having everything else shipped." Meggie remembered her manners—and changed the subject at the same time. "Come on in." She stepped back and gestured toward the living room.

Dolores took her lower lip between her even teeth. "Oh, Mr. Bravo never lets anyone in." Her black eyes gleamed with bright interest. "But now, it is your apartment, too, *sí*?"

"*Sí*. Now, come on." She took Dolores's arm and

pulled her into the hall, then closed the door behind her. She led the way to the living room. "Have a seat."

Dolores perched on the end of one of the sapphire sofas. Her dark gaze scanned the room. "Very nice," she said, sighing and smiling, as if the room gave her physical pleasure.

"Yes," said Meggie. "I think so, too."

"So." Dolores folded her plump hands in her ample lap. "You will come to dinner *a mi casa?*"

"Well, I..."

"We would be so pleased to have you."

Meggie grinned. "All right. I'd love it."

That night, Meggie met Dolores's sweet, quiet husband, Benny, as well as two of the Garnicas' grandchildren.

"This is Yolanda. We call her 'Yolie,'" Dolores said of a slim, serious girl with a trigonometry book under one arm and a pencil behind her ear. "She lives here, with Benito and me. She is fourteen and a genius."

"Oh, Grandma," Yolie protested, her face coloring prettily. "Don't."

"But it's only the truth. You are *muy lista,* one very smart girl." Dolores turned to a tall, leanly muscled young man with black curly hair, a devilish smile and eyes of a startling blue. "And this is my Mateo. He comes just for dinner. He is becoming a great movie star. Too bad that he thinks he must call himself 'Matt Shane.'"

"I'm an *actor,* Grandma, not a movie star," the young man corrected with somewhat strained affection. "'Matt' is short for Mateo. And Shane *is* my real name."

Dolores made a disgusted sound. "The name of that

terrible man who broke your poor mama's heart. He does not deserve to have his name in the movies when you become a famous star.''

''Grandma, give it up. It's *my* name. I don't even think of it as his.'' Dolores made more disapproving sounds as Mateo turned that gorgeous smile on Meggie. ''Call me 'Matt.' And welcome to L.A.''

Dolores slapped him on the arm. ''She is a married woman. You watch yourself.''

The next morning, Dolores showed Meggie the coin laundry in the building next door and explained that the tenants in both buildings used it. She also gave Meggie directions to the supermarket several blocks away, and walked her down to Pahlavi's, the corner store, where a loaf of bread or a quart of milk could be bought if she didn't feel like driving all the way to the supermarket.

In the afternoon, Meggie went shopping. As she pushed her cart up and down the aisles, she saw a lot of ordinary-looking people like herself, wearing ordinary clothes with hair of ordinary colors: blond, brown, auburn and black. She also saw a woman with silver rings in her lips and her nose and a man all in leather with tattoos covering his arms to his elbows. She saw a lot of young people wearing black, with spiky hair of green or purple.

L.A. was a place of great diversity, Meggie decided. People came in all colors here. They spoke with a variety of accents. It made getting the groceries into something of an event.

Later, Meggie met the Tyrells, an ebony-skinned couple in their fifties. Their apartment shared a landing with Nate's. The Tyrells came out of their door just as Meggie was bringing her groceries in. She introduced herself.

"Lovely to meet you," said Mrs. Tyrell, who looked absolutely stunning in a white linen dress.

"Charmed," said her husband. He wore an immaculately tailored black three-piece suit, complete with a gold watch chain hanging from his vest pocket.

As they exchanged pleasantries, Meggie caught a glimpse inside their door, which had a tiny foyer that opened right onto the living room. She saw an oppressive abundance of heavy, dark, ornately carved furniture.

"If you should need anything...*anything,* please feel free to call us," Mrs. Tyrell insisted as Mr. Tyrell closed and locked the door.

Meggie promised that she would and then watched, bemused, as the regal pair turned and descended the stairs.

The next day, Wednesday, Meggie met Bob and Ted, a screenwriter and a caterer's assistant, who shared the apartment beneath Nate's. She also introduced herself to Peg Tolly, an exotic dancer with enormous breasts, who had a one-bedroom upstairs around the opposite side of the building. Below Peg lived Edie Benson, who had once been a nurse and now rolled an oxygen tank around with her wherever she went, due to her steadily worsening case of emphysema. Meggie met Edie on a quick trip down to the corner to buy some butter, which she'd forgotten to pick up at the supermarket the day before. The older woman had just toddled out to the sidewalk with her oxygen tank on its little rollers, when Meggie came dashing out herself.

After introductions had been accomplished, Edie confessed that she was headed to the corner market, too.

"I'm just going down to pick up my special little sandwich," Edie panted. "Mr. Pahlavi always makes it for me." The store's owner ran a sandwich counter in back of the store, by the beverage cases.

Meggie offered to get the sandwich for her.

"No, no. Can't have that. I like to do for myself. That's how I am."

So they walked together, picking their way carefully over the cracks and humps in the sidewalk, stopping now and then for Edie to catch her breath, down to the bottom of the street and into the cramped, dim store run by Mr. Pahlavi.

That night, Meggie invited the Garnicas over and served them chicken with dumplings, the way her grandma Kane used to make it. Benny remarked that the dish could use a few jalapeños, but was otherwise delicious. Meggie enjoyed their company, though she felt a certain anxiety all evening. Nate was due back any time now. He would very likely return that night.

All through dinner, and later, as she got ready for bed, she kept thinking of the answering machine in Nate's office. She had heard the phone ring in there more than once over the past two days. She knew his machine was taking the calls. Nate had a small remote device that he used to pick up his messages from an outside phone. She kept picturing him calling from a phone booth or that cell phone of his, beeping for his messages, listening to them play. She had a burning desire to go in there, to sit in the chair behind his desk and snatch the phone from its cradle the minute it rang. Maybe she would catch him calling in. She could tell him she was here, waiting for him.

But then, if it wasn't him, she'd only be interfering with his message system. And he probably wouldn't think much of that. So somehow, she restrained herself from answering his business phone.

Nate didn't return that night. Meggie woke early the next morning to find herself alone in Nate's big bed.

After a quick trip to the bathroom, she returned to the bed, pulled the covers up around her and reached for the phone on the black-lacquer nightstand. She punched out Sonny's number. Farrah answered on the second ring. Meggie asked her how things were going. Farrah reported that the mercury had dipped below zero again last night and as soon as it warmed up a few degrees, Sonny would be heading out to check on the heifers in the South Pasture.

"We're watching the ground freeze around here, Meggie," Farrah said. "We can handle it without you, believe me."

"I know. I just…feel a little homesick, I guess. And I miss you all."

Farrah made a tender sound. "And we miss you, too. But it's only for a few months, right? And then you and Nate will be back here at home where you belong."

Meggie pulled the covers a little closer around her. She considered herself an honest person. Yet, in a day or two, she'd be flying home with some trumped-up story about how things hadn't worked out between her and Nate. Nate would look like the bad guy. And Farrah and Sonny would feel sorry for poor Meggie, pregnant and deserted by the man who, they believed, had promised to stand beside her until death.

"Meggie, are you all right?" Farrah asked after the silence went on too long.

"Fine. And yes, I'll be glad when we get home for good." That was the truth, more or less. Meggie slid her hand under the covers and laid it on her stomach, which was beginning to round out the tiniest bit. She would be part of a "we" when she went home, because Nate's baby would be with her.

"You need some kind of project," Farrah said briskly. "You know how you are."

Meggie smiled and relaxed a little. "No, how am I?"

"A *doer*. So don't let yourself sit around just because you're in the big city. Find something to keep yourself busy."

Meggie heard herself agreeing before she stopped to think that she didn't really have time for a project; in a day or so, she'd be out of there. Right then, from Farrah's end of the line, Meggie heard a loud, outraged wail.

"Oops," said Farrah. "Davey wants Mommy. Gotta go."

Meggie told Farrah to kiss the crying toddler for her, said goodbye and headed for the kitchen to rustle up some breakfast.

Meggie ate to the sounds of L.A.: horns honking, someone shouting out on the street, a siren in the distance, coming closer and then fading off again. She watched the sun come up over the carports, spilling its hot orange light in the kitchen window, over the yellow lilies and across the wall to the black and white tile. As she stared at the lilies, with the sun on their freckled petals, a wave of longing moved through her. She wanted Nate—and dreaded his return at the same time.

Somehow, she got through the endless day, reading a little, walking down to Pahlavi's with Edie around noon. In the afternoon, to keep busy, she baked cookies, *lots* of cookies. The smell of them baking soothed her; it was something she would have done at home, this time of year, with a blizzard blowing outside and a roaring fire in the stove.

Once the cookies were done, she took them around to the other tenants in the building. Everyone was sweetly appreciative. Even Peg, who said she couldn't eat them, seemed pleased at the effort Meggie had put in.

"Well, honey, this is real nice. But a fat exotic dancer is an unemployed exotic dancer, you hear what I'm saying?" She thought a minute, tapping a long crimson nail against her front teeth. "You know, though, a lot of men got a yen for a little home cookin'. So how about if I take these babies to work with me tonight and pass them around?"

"Good idea," Meggie agreed, trying her best not to gape at Peg's breasts, which besides being huge, were very high and rounded. They seemed to float out from her chest, hard, perfect spheres, totally defiant of gravity.

That night, Meggie hardly slept at all. Every slightest sound had her eyes popping open. Then she'd stare into the darkness, straining her ears to hear if it was Nate coming home.

But it wasn't. She woke before dawn, still alone, and decided she'd had enough of trying to sleep.

She ate a light breakfast and tried to think of something to do with herself to make the time pass. Since her meager wardrobe needed washing, she put on a pair of Nate's black sweats and an old L.A. Lakers T-shirt that she found in one of his drawers and carried her own clothes next door to the laundry room. The sky beyond the carports had just started to pinken when she got the wash cycle going.

Someone had left a tattered copy of *People* magazine

on one of the chairs, so Meggie settled in to read about Julia Roberts. She was studying the photos that accompanied the article, trying to decide whether the actress looked better with her hair short or long, when Meggie heard strange noises coming through the wall behind her—bumps and grunts and the sound of furniture toppling. Meggie tried not to listen, tried to concentrate harder on the news about Julia and how she was overcoming divorce and career difficulties.

A sharp, pained cry from the other side of the wall mobilized her. Someone in there was getting beat up. Bad.

Meggie dropped the magazine and jumped from her chair, which she took in both hands and hurled against the wall. Then she shouted, at the top of her lungs, "Help! Police! Fire! Police!" She grabbed a second chair and hurled it, too. "Fire! Police! Help!"

She waited. There was dead silence from the other side of the wall. Meggie shouted again, "I know who you are, and I've called the police!"

That did it. She heard a door slam, and footsteps pounding away. She ran out in time to see a thin male figure in jeans and a mesh shirt disappear around the front of the building. A door stood open a few feet away—the door to the apartment that shared a wall with the laundry room.

Meggie peered inside, through a tiny hall. The living room beyond the hall was chaos, a welter of overturned furniture, broken lamps and ripped cushions. Meggie heard a pitiful moan.

Her feet moved of their own accord, carrying her over the threshold and down the short length of the hall. A slender man, who might have been anywhere from forty to sixty, lay on the floor in the corner. He seemed to be covered in blood.

"Please," he whimpered. "Take the money. Take the money and go...."

Meggie spotted the phone on the floor beneath a broken chair. She picked it up: still working. She dialed 911. When she'd completed the call, she knelt beside the bleeding man to see if there was anything she could do for him.

A cursory examination led her to suspect that all the blood had come from a couple of scalp wounds and a number of minor cuts, many of them on the poor man's face. But it didn't look as if any major artery had been sliced. She tried to make him comfortable, sliding a pillow under his head and a blanket over him, since he'd already started shaking with shock.

She was sponging his face with a moist cloth, trying to wipe off a little of the blood without disturbing any of the cuts, when the paramedics arrived. They drove the white ambulance van down the driveway between the buildings and into the parking lot by the carports.

All the commotion brought Dolores and Benny. Edie came, too, toddling along with her oxygen tank, and Peg, still in her bathrobe, as well as Bob, the screenwriter, and a few other people Meggie didn't know. Dolores let out a stream of frantic Spanish at the sight of one of her tenants so badly used. She clung to Benny.

"Ah, *Dios mio,* it is a bad world sometimes! Poor Señor Leverson. A quiet man, *muy amable.* Did he ever hurt a fly? No, never. But the bad ones, they come and do the bad things to him anyway...."

It was full daylight and the paramedics were loading the injured man into the ambulance when the police car turned into the driveway. The two patrolmen inside took one look at all the blood on the Lakers T-shirt Meggie wore and decided to take her statement first.

She explained who she was, what she had heard, what she had done and what she had seen. The ambulance drove away. The tall, blond patrolman who had questioned her began congratulating her on her cool head and quick response in a crisis.

Right then, a black sports car turned into the driveway and rolled toward them. It was Nate.

Chapter Seven

Nate swung the sports car into the space next to the blue Volvo. Then he jumped out and slammed the door.

Meggie's heart lifted as she watched him stride toward her. He looked so handsome, in rumpled khakis and a midnight-blue polo shirt. There were circles under his eyes, though. He'd probably been going without sleep—on a stakeout, or something.

Just as Nate reached Meggie's side, the older of the two patrolmen, Officer Rinkley, came out of Mr. Leverson's apartment. He strolled over and stood next to his young partner, folding his arms across his chest. "Hello, Bravo."

"Rinkley." Nate dipped his head in a brief, ironic nod.

It surprised Meggie that they knew each other. But then she realized that in Nate's line of work, he probably crossed paths with a lot of policemen.

Nate turned to Meggie, his dark eyes running a quick, ruthless inventory of the sweats and T-shirt she'd borrowed from him—and the blood all over them. "What the hell's going on?"

The younger officer launched into a glowing account of Meggie's bravery in rescuing a helpless man from assault by a burglar. Nate cut him off in midsentence by turning to Meggie. "Are you hurt?"

"Oh, no. I'm fine. Really, I just—"

He grabbed her hand. His touch felt wonderful. But his scowl worried her a little. "So you're done with her, then?" he said to the officers.

Rinkley shrugged. "Sure. We know how to reach her if we need her for anything more."

"Good." He cast Meggie another dark look. "Let's go."

"But, Nate, I—"

"Meggie. Inside. Now."

"But I've got laundry. I need to—"

Nate turned to Dolores, who still stood with Benny and the others, not far away. "Dolores, will you take care of her damn laundry? Please."

Dolores drew herself up. "I would be honored to care for her laundry."

"Thank you."

"De nada."

Nate yanked on Meggie's hand. She stumbled after him, feeling a little foolish and a lot bewildered, across the parking lot to the stairs that led up to Nate's door.

Terrified and furious, Nate dragged Meggie in the door, shoved it closed and turned the dead bolt. Then he backed her up against the wall, took her sweet face in his hands and demanded, "What the hell is wrong with you?"

Her brows drew together. "Nothing. Nate, I—"

"You've got blood on your chin." He scrubbed at it with his thumb, frantic, scared to death at what might have happened to her.

She shook her head, trying to escape his hold. "Nate—"

But he wasn't letting her go. "Meggie. This isn't Medicine Creek. You can't just jump into the middle of things here, understand? You could get yourself killed."

"That poor man needed help."

"Meggie—"

"I'm not going to apologize for what I did, Nate. I would do it again. In a heartbeat." She gave him one of those hard, level looks that seared right through him. "And so would you."

"I'm different."

"How?"

"I'm—"

"A man," she sneered.

"Meggie, listen to me—"

She put a hand on his chest, firmly, to hold his attention on what she was about to say. "No. You listen. I've been doing a man's work since I was a kid. I know how to handle myself. And I am not a fool. All I did was scare the guy off."

"Meggie—"

"I'm not done. When someone's in trouble, I help them if I can. Whether I'm in L.A. or Timbuktu."

He knew that look in her eye, knew she wouldn't budge on this. He drew in a long, steadying breath and let it out slowly. Then he released her, stepped back and slumped against the wall opposite her. They regarded each other across the width of the narrow hall.

"You were scared for me," she said after a moment. "That's nice."

"It is not nice. Not nice at all."

"You look tired," she said softly.

"It was a grim job."

"Tell me all about it."

"Maybe later." He looked her up and down, wondering how it was possible to be so damn glad to see someone. "You're a bloody mess."

She lifted her chin and grinned. "It's good to see you, too."

"When did you get here?"

"Monday."

Four days. For four days she'd been here, waiting for him. If he'd called on his private line, she probably would have answered. The idea pleased him. Too much.

He asked, "Other than having to prevent a murder, how have you been getting along?"

"Just fine. Dolores is great. And everyone—all your neighbors—have been sweet to me."

"Good." He reached out and took her hand again, but this time gently. "Come on. You need a bath."

She went along, as docile as a lamb, into the bathroom with him. He ran the water and removed her bloodstained clothes and guided her down into the big tub. When all the blood was washed away, he bundled her in a towel and carried her to his bed, where he laid her down and peeled the towel from her.

He looked at her, lying on his own bed, where he had never dared to dream he would have her. Her still-damp hair was spread out across his pillows. He loved the full, womanly curves of her body, the deep breasts and the slightly rounded belly, the soft, thick triangle of curls between her long, strong legs.

She reached up her arms. "Nate. Come here to me."

He went on looking at her—as he quickly removed every stitch he was wearing. She sighed when at last he bent down to her. Her arms twined around his neck and he stretched out along the soft, waiting length of her.

"I wasn't sure you'd be here," he confessed against her lips.

"I'm here." She kissed him through the words.

"Yeah. I can feel it."

She shifted slightly, parting her thighs, lifting her body in clear invitation. He slid between them—and home.

She moaned into his mouth.

He took the sound, tasted it, found it satisfying in a way no other woman's moans had ever been. She wrapped her legs around him. They began the long, slow dance that he always wished might never end.

At the end, he pressed in deep and she held him. So close. So complete. So exactly as lovemaking always should be.

Afterward, they just lay there, talking, filling each other in on the past few days. He told her a little about the divorce case he'd been working on, a surveillance deal down in Baja, where he had to hide in the hibiscus bushes outside a bungalow love nest, taking pictures of a certain wealthy, famous woman and her cabana-boy lover. The whole thing had depressed him. He had to turn in the pictures and the report at the Bel Air mansion of the woman's husband that afternoon.

Meggie talked about Dolores and the other tenants in his building. He had to smile when he learned that she knew all of them already. He'd lived there for five years and had done no more than exchange perfunctory greetings with a few of them.

She fell silent, lying there so peacefully, with her head on his chest. She stroked his arm in an idle, affectionate way and he thought it wouldn't be half-bad to just lie there with her like that for about a century.

"Nate?"

"Um?"

"The paramedics said that Mr. Leverson will probably be all right."

"Leverson?"

"The man from the building next door, the one who got beat up."

"Right. Well, good."

"They were taking him to Cedars Sinai Hospital. They said it's not far from here. I think I'll...go visit him, tomorrow."

Something in her tone bothered him, a hesitation, as if she had another issue entirely on her mind, beyond the injured man and a visit to Cedars.

"Okay?" she asked, still hesitant.

Maybe she thought he might tell her no and they'd end up in another argument. Well, she didn't have to worry on that score. If he couldn't talk her out of playing hero, he certainly wouldn't waste his time trying to convince her not to visit some beat-up burglary victim.

"Nate? Is that okay with you?"

He shrugged. "Fine. If that's what you want to do."

"It is." She lifted her head enough to plant a kiss on his chest, then lay back down again. "And Nate, I've been thinking..."

He chuckled. "Oh, no."

She slid off his chest and scooted up onto the pillow,

bracing her head on her hand so she could meet his eyes. "What does that mean, 'Oh, no'?"

"Forget I said it. Think all you want."

"Thank you very much." Her thick, dark hair, shot with strands of gold and red, tumbled around her face; her wide eyes gleamed with humor.

He kissed the nose she'd wrinkled up at him. "All right. What have you been thinking?"

"I read an article a few months ago—in *Newsweek* or *Time,* I think. I can't remember where for sure, really. Anyway, it was an article about neighbors in big cities banding together, organizing themselves to look out for each other."

He knew what she was talking about. "You mean Community Watch?"

"Right. That's it. They had an eight-hundred number you could call, to have someone come and explain how to go about it."

"Why am I picturing meetings in my living room?"

"Maybe because there are going to *be* meetings in your living room." She reached out, pulled him close against her soft breasts. He went without reluctance, sucker that he was for her. She held him in her arms and stroked his hair. "Nate, I'd like to call that number. I'd like to get everybody in this building and the one next door organized. I'd like to know they can look out for each other. Is that all right with you?"

He made a low sound of agreement.

She went on stroking his hair. "I'd like to help them be safe, before I leave here."

There it was again, that strange tone. He pulled back and met her eyes. "What's wrong?"

She bit her lip, shook her head. "Nothing. I just...I

really like all the people here. I don't want to see them hurt.''

He swore low. ''Meggie. It's okay. If you want Community Watch, you can have Community Watch.''

She grabbed him then and hugged him hard. He felt like a million bucks. When she let him go, he realized he was starving. ''What's in the kitchen?''

She laughed. ''A stove. A refrigerator. A sink. Counters.''

''I mean in the way of food.''

''Eggs. Milk. Bread. The usual.''

He was already tossing back the covers, reaching for his slacks. He looked around at her. She hadn't budged from the bed. ''Come on. Get dressed. I want some breakfast.''

''I've had mine.''

''Then come watch me eat.''

''Nate?''

He zipped up his pants, then lifted an eyebrow at her.

''Could I borrow another pair of sweats, maybe, and a shirt?''

''Sure.'' He gestured at the bureau. ''Help yourself.'' He pulled on his shirt. Then he watched as she jumped from the bed, found some sweats, put them on and tied the drawstring, her pretty breasts bouncing temptingly as she moved. Damn, she was beautiful. It seemed to him that she got softer and riper looking every time he looked at her. ''Meggie?''

''Um?''

''Where are your own clothes?''

She looked up, blinked and pushed her hair away from her face. Then she turned to the bureau again and opened another drawer. ''Dolores has all my things.'' She took out a T-shirt and pulled it over her head. ''The laundry, remember?" She flipped her hair free at the neck.

"Everything you brought with you was dirty already?"

"Well. Yes. I didn't bring much. I...hate checking my suitcase at the airport. I'm afraid they'll lose it. And besides, I thought while I was here I might pick up a few things. I'll have to cart them back with me, but I could use some new clothes."

Her explanation made perfect sense. And he had no idea why he'd made such a big deal out of it, anyway. "Whatever. Now, are you ready? I'm starving."

She beamed at him. "Lead the way."

Meggie went to see Mr. Leverson the next day. He was conscious. The nurses told her before she went into his room that he would be released in a day or two.

He smiled at her through his bandages and asked her to call him by his first name, which was Hector. "Thank you, young lady. You saved my life."

Meggie took his thin, bruised hand.

"My home is destroyed, isn't it?" He sounded as if he might cry.

Meggie hastened to reassure him. "No. No, really. It's pretty messed up, but nothing a new sofa, some lamps and a little paint won't fix."

"I have no family," Hector confessed in a whisper. "My wife died ten years ago. And we were childless. But I have good insurance—I've been careful about that. I wonder..." His voice trailed off.

"What? Come on. Tell me, please."

"It's too much to ask."

"No. It's not. Come on. Ask me."

"Well, I'd like to get my insurance company moving on this. But from the hospital, it's a little difficult."

"Would you like me to call them? Dolores and I could show them the damage to your apartment."

"Oh. Would you?"

Meggie smiled. "I'd be glad to."

Nate called her a pushover when she got home. But when Hector's insurance company gave her the run-around, Nate took the phone and bullied the insurance agent until the man agreed to send someone over that afternoon.

The agent showed up right at five. Dolores and Meggie worked on him together, leading him through the trashed apartment, bemoaning the pain poor Hector had suffered.

Before he left, the agent promised that all Hector needed to do was send him the receipts for the cost of the repairs. On Saturday, Meggie, Nate and Benny cleaned the place up and painted the living room and kitchen. The intruder had never entered the single bedroom or the bath, so they remained intact. By Saturday evening, the apartment looked fresh and new. The living room lacked furniture, but Hector could handle that problem himself, with the money from his insurance company.

Hector returned home on Monday morning. Dolores and Meggie took the blue Volvo to get him. When they helped him inside and he saw what his landlady and neighbors had done, he sat down on the one chair left at his table and cried. Dolores clucked over him and told him not to upset himself, that they had all been happy to help out.

He wanted to get out his checkbook right then. Dolores reassured him that they could settle up later.

"Money isn't enough anyway," Hector protested. "What else can I do to repay you?"

"Come to the Community Watch meeting tonight," Meggie replied. "At my apartment, next door."

Amos Abel, the volunteer counselor from Community Watch, came to speak to the tenants of Nate's building at seven that night. Everyone in the building showed up, as well as four people from the building where Hector lived. Hector came, too, his face still bandaged, his left leg so stiff that Benny had to help him up the stairs.

Meggie and Dolores provided coffee and cookies. Amos Abel passed around brochures that explained the steps to a safe neighborhood. He advised them to tell each other their schedules, to learn each other's routines and to try to have one person in each building keeping an eye out at all times.

"I know, I know," Mr. Abel said. "You have to sleep sometimes. But do your best. Be aware. There is no substitute for vigilance." He gestured around the room. "And this—all of you here together, getting to know each other—is the first and most important step. People who know each other look out for each other. They take action when something seems strange in a neighbor's apartment." He advised the tenants on the ground floor to consider barring their windows. "I realize some of you just don't want to live that way. But you must understand that an unbarred ground-floor window is virtually impossible to truly secure."

Before he left, Amos gave them all Community Watch stickers to put on their doors and in their windows, explaining, "The idea is to let the bad guys know that this is a place where people look out for each other.'' He also gave Dolores signs to put up in front of the buildings. The tenants agreed to meet again on Thursday, to exchange schedules.

Meggie felt pretty good by the time they all returned to their own apartments. She dared to hope that maybe, working together, they could protect themselves against predators like the one who had attacked Hector.

"Proud of yourself, aren't you?" Nate teased, after the meeting, when they lay together in bed.

With a small, abashed groan, she snuggled in closer to him.

"Oh, now you're going modest on me.'' He started to tickle her.

She laughed and squirmed and batted his hands away. And then he kissed her. She kept on squirming, but for an entirely different reason—and she stopped trying to push him away.

Later, while Nate slept, Meggie lay wide-awake. The inner glow she'd felt at helping Nate's neighbors had somehow turned to a guilty heat down deep inside her.

She had come here to L.A. for one reason: to tell Nate face-to-face about the baby.

But instead, she had only lied some more. And Nate, whose ebony eyes always saw through the cleverest deceptions, seemed totally oblivious to the lies she told—lies she would not stop telling for as long as he continued to believe them.

Meggie understood herself now. All her vows to the contrary, she would go on lying until Nate finally couldn't help but see the truth; until her own thickening waistline at last betrayed her. She would steal every glorious moment with him, each last second that God was willing to give her.

Just a little while longer, she whispered silently to

herself, *here, in this place of palm trees and odd, sweet people. A little while longer. With Nate. Is it too much to ask?*

Meggie knew it *was* too much to ask; her agreement with Nate called for her to let him go as soon as she got pregnant. But she just didn't care. She would continue her deception with evasions and half lies. Gentle lies, she told herself. Lies that hurt no one, really. Lies that only bought her a little more precious time with Nate.

Nate left again on Wednesday, after warning Meggie that he probably wouldn't return until the weekend. As soon as he was gone, she looked up an ob-gyn in the phone book. On Thursday morning, she went to see him. He told her she was well over three months pregnant and doing just fine. He asked for urine and blood samples, then said that the office would call her if there were any abnormalities in the tests.

Meggie knew a moment of panic. What if they called and Nate answered?

But then calm descended. If Nate answered, so be it. Her foolish deception couldn't go on forever anyway. And she owed it to their baby to get decent prenatal care.

After she left the doctor's office, Meggie went shopping, as she'd told Nate she would. She bought some underwear, T-shirts, two loose jumpers and three pairs of jeans with elastic waists, clothes that she would be able to wear through most of her pregnancy—clothes that would also help to disguise her condition for a while. As a pure indulgence, she also picked up a bottle of perfume that smelled of roses. She smiled to herself as she sniffed it on her wrist, picturing Nate kissing all her pulse points, whispering that she smelled like a rose.

She got back to the apartment at four-thirty, but all she did was drop her shopping bags inside the door. She needed to pay a quick visit to Dolores, so they could talk about the refreshments for the Community Watch meeting that night.

However, Dolores wasn't in the mood to discuss refreshments. She opened the door with eyes red from crying. "*Hola*, Meggie," she said miserably.

"Dolores. What's wrong?"

"Come in." She turned and left Meggie to follow after.

In the kitchen, Dolores dropped to a chair by the table in front of a tissue box and a pile of used tissues. A sob shook her plump shoulders. She ripped a tissue from the box and buried her face in it.

Meggie went straight to her and laid a comforting hand on her shoulder, which inspired Dolores to erupt from her chair and into Meggie's bewildered arms.

"Ah, sweet virgin, oh *Dios mio. Mi familia—¿dónde está?* Where is my family, Megan? *Todos mis niños*, where have they gone?"

Meggie soothed and clucked and looked around frantically for Benny. "It's okay. It's all right. Settle down, now. Where's Benny?"

Dolores moaned. "He goes. Whenever I get like this. I give him the ache in *la cabeza*, the head, you know?" Dolores wailed some more.

Meggie hugged her and patted her until she settled down. Then she sat her back in her chair and took the one next to her. "All right, now. What is it?"

A long, rambling, Spanish-punctuated explanation ensued. Dolores had borne her Benny five beautiful

children—two sons and three daughters—all of them
citizens of this great land. Between them, all those children had given Dolores and Benny eleven handsome
grandchildren. Yet, out of all those children and all
those grandchildren, only one—Yolie—would be home
for Thanksgiving. Even Mateo, who always came, was
off on the road somewhere, playing a gang leader in
West Side Story.

When the sad tale had been told, Meggie sympathized
some more. And then it occurred to her that they could
share Thanksgiving together: Dolores, Benny and Yolanda—and Meggie and Nate. She suggested the idea
to Dolores, who actually started to smile through her
tears.

Then Meggie had an even better suggestion. "Wait.
We could invite everyone. In the two buildings. That
way no one would have to spend the holiday alone."

Dolores declared it a brilliant idea. "A fiesta. *Una
celebración grande*. For all the lonely ones. For everyone. ¿*Sí*? Yes. Wonderful!"

They had the menu half planned by the time Dolores
promised to bring cookies to the meeting that night and
Meggie took her leave.

Nate returned ahead of schedule, on Friday afternoon.
After a lovely hour in bed, Meggie told him all the
news. He groaned when he heard how several of his
neighbors would be coming to his place for dinner next
Thursday, but he didn't try to change her plans.

The days that followed were happy ones. Nate took
Meggie out for a little sight-seeing. They walked down
Hollywood Boulevard, hand in hand, reading the names
of the stars on the sidewalk, looking in the windows of
the rather rundown stores, all decorated for Christmas

now, in shiny red garlands and twinkling party lights. They visited the Descanso Gardens, where there were roses blooming even now, in November. They took in a movie at Mann's Chinese. And Dolores had tickets to a Sunday matinee at the Mark Taper Forum, a new play starring one of her grandson's friends. She and Benny didn't feel like going, so Meggie and Nate went, instead.

On Monday, Nate spent a few hours in his office at his computer, then he went out to meet with a client. He came back with the news that he'd be leaving Tuesday.

Meggie's heart sank. "For how long?"

He grinned. "Don't want me to miss the big feast, huh?"

She sighed. "You're right. I really want you here."

"Settle down." He came and put his arms around her. "This thing will take a day and a half, max. I have to serve some papers to a guy in Crescent City, up near the Oregon border. I know right where to find him, and he's going nowhere from what my client told me, so I don't even have to go looking."

"What are you saying?"

"That I promise I'll be back Wednesday at the latest, Tuesday night if I'm lucky. I wouldn't miss your Thanksgiving—you know that."

The next morning, Nate tried to get Meggie to sleep in. But she wouldn't. She insisted on getting up with him at 4 a.m. to fix him some breakfast before he took off.

She had set the timer the night before, so the coffee was already made. Nate offered to help fix the food, but she wouldn't hear of it. So he sat at the table, letting her wait on him, sipping caffeine and watching her bustle around in his bathrobe, whipping up eggs and toast.

He loved to watch her. He thought that she could do just about anything. She was equally at home treating cattle and baking cookies for her Community Watch meetings. She could pull on her Wranglers and eat dust in the drag during a trail drive—or put on her party duds and dance until dawn.

Even the few pounds she'd been putting on lately looked good on her. She seemed softer, rounder, sexier than ever.

Right then, she stood on tiptoe, reaching inside the cabinet above the stove to bring down the little bowl she liked to use for serving jam. Her slightly rounded belly pressed against the counter rim.

Something shifted inside Nate at that precise moment. And he saw the truth he'd been managing not to see.

Meggie was pregnant.

Chapter Eight

Meggie found the little bowl, closed the cupboard and set the bowl on the small section of counter between the stove and the refrigerator. She spooned out the jam. Then she put the jam jar away and took the bowl to the table. She looked up and smiled at Nate as she set the bowl down. "More coffee?"

He returned her smile mechanically, shaking his head. "I'm fine."

With a tiny shrug of her shoulders, she went back to the stove to stir the eggs. The toast popped up. She buttered it, put it on a small plate and cut it into neat triangles.

Nate went on watching her, stunned. In the space of one brief second, everything had changed. She set the food before him and a smaller portion at her own place, then went about brewing herself some herbal tea.

Herbal tea. It came to him that he hadn't seen her

drink coffee in weeks—maybe months. But that made sense. Caffeine couldn't be that good for the baby.

When the tea was ready, she carried it to the table and sat down opposite him. She took a bite of egg and looked up. Before she could ask why he wasn't eating, he picked up his own fork and began putting eggs in his mouth. As he dutifully chewed the eggs and ate the toast, she talked about her Thanksgiving party, about who would be there and how she would seat them all.

Nate watched her mouth move, nodded at the right places and made interested noises when required.

He said nothing at all about what he'd just realized—no doubt for the same reason she hadn't: because as soon as they got it out in the open, there would be no more reason for them to go on sleeping together, go on *being* together.

He had a ridiculous urge to throw back his head and laugh out loud at his own ability to deceive himself. Talk about clues....

He recalled all those menstrual periods she never seemed to have. And all the times when he would glance up to find her watching him with a strange, guilty look on her face. He remembered the way she sometimes stayed awake nights—fretting, he knew, by the stiff, bottled-up way she lay beside him.

He might have asked her, "What's on your mind?"

But he hadn't.

Because he hadn't wanted to know.

Meggie happily chattered on. "There's a party rental place a few blocks down on Santa Monica. I can get long folding tables from them, and good, sturdy folding chairs with padded seats. Not to mention table linens. Mrs. Tyrell is letting us use her china, glassware and silver."

She paused, but only for a sip of tea. Then she continued, "The Tyrells have gorgeous stuff, Nate. You should see it. Plates with gold rims and cut-crystal goblets. Mrs. Tyrell seemed really pleased to contribute them to the party. The table will be beautiful—just you wait. I've ordered a turkey, a really big one. Fresh, not frozen. And I'm going to go ahead and spring for a spiral-cut ham, because I think people like a choice...."

Damn. This was bad. This was trouble. This was exactly the reason he had kept himself clear of her for all those years. Because she was a woman who could make wearing a ball and chain seem like a great idea.

And maybe it was. Just not for him.

Nate had spent most of his childhood living over the bar his mother owned in Cheyenne. Sharilyn Tickberry Bravo hadn't been the most attentive of mothers; she worked nights and slept days. She had the bar to run, after all, because Nate's father—Bad Clint, as everyone called him—was not the kind of man a woman could depend on.

But Nate hadn't minded. He'd *liked* things that way. He'd gone where he wanted and kept his own hours from about the age of five on.

At fourteen, he'd gone to live at the Rising Sun. Under protest. He'd gotten used to it after a year or two. He'd even ended up forging strong bonds with his grandfather and his cousins. And Edna and her family, too. But those bonds didn't hold him there, with the Bravos; no bonds could hold him. Even at the Rising Sun, he'd only been marking time—until he was eighteen and could be free.

He left the ranch not long after he graduated from high school. He'd lived in a lot of places since then and acquired a number of disparate skills. He'd even put himself through four years of college, though few people knew that.

But most of all, he'd kept himself free. Nate was a man who needed to live free. It was something bred in the bone, this hunger to stay free. His mother had it. And so had Bad Clint.

And nothing, not even big-eyed Meggie May Kane and that baby she just had to have, would make him start thinking about settling down.

"Is something wrong, Nate?" She'd stopped chattering and started watching him across the table, those incredible eyes just a little bit troubled.

Yeah, I just noticed you're pregnant, he thought. "No, nothing," he said. "Why?"

"You seem...quiet, all of a sudden."

"Just thinking." He pushed back his chair. "And it's time I got out of here."

"Oh, Nate..." She looked adorably sad at his leaving.

More reason to get out quick.

They had a few things to talk about. But not now. He had to go now. They could face the music when he returned.

Before or after the big Thanksgiving feast? a voice in his mind taunted.

Ignoring that voice, he carried his plate to the sink, ran some water in it and then kept on going, back to the bedroom, where he had his bag already packed. He pulled on his jacket, scooped up the bag and headed out.

She was waiting for him by the front door. "I'll miss you." Her soft, warm body leaned toward him.

And he couldn't stop from dropping his bag and reaching for her. He pulled her close and settled his mouth over hers. She twined her arms around his neck. She tasted of peppermint tea and jam. And she smelled like a rose.

It took everything he had in him to pull away. "Lock up after me."

"I will. I promise." She watched him pick up his bag once more. "Come back by Thanksgiving."

"Right. Gotta go." He drew back the chain, turned the dead bolt and opened the door. The brisk predawn air greeted him. He stepped onto the landing and then ran down the stairs.

He knew she stood there in the doorway, watching until he disappeared, though he never turned to look back.

Nate flew to San Francisco and rented a car to take him up the coast to Crescent City. There, he discovered that the guy who wasn't going anywhere had decided to spend Thanksgiving in Chicago. Nate got out his cell phone and called his client, who reiterated that cost was not a factor and he wanted those papers served yesterday. Nate called the airlines and managed to get a seat on a flight out of San Francisco. And then he hopped in his rental car and drove like hell to get back there in time. He made the call he dreaded as he sped down the coast highway.

As soon as she picked up the phone, he laid it on her. "It turns out I've got to fly to Chicago."

Meggie's disappointment came at him through the silence on the line, as palpable as any words would have been.

"Dammit, Meggie. I have to work."

He heard her sigh. "I know." Then she made her

voice pleasantly brisk. "Any chance you might make it back for Thanksgiving?"

"How the hell should I know?"

Another reproachful beat of silence, then she said, "Don't be mad at me, Nate."

"I'm not."

"You sound—"

"Meggie."

"What?"

"I'll try to get there for your party. That's the most I can do."

She sighed again. "Okay."

"I have to go now." He didn't, but talking to her only reminded him of all the things they needed to say.

"All right. Nate?"

"Yeah?"

"Just…" She seemed not to know what to say. "Be safe," she finished at last, rather listlessly.

"I will." He disconnected the call and tossed the phone on the empty seat beside him, wondering what in hell had ever possessed him to imagine that this whole crazy plot would work out. One way or another, it was a setup for heartbreak.

He understood Meggie. To the very soul of her. He knew that for almost twenty years she'd maintained an irrational attachment to him. And he'd always been scrupulously careful not to encourage her.

Until he'd managed to let himself get roped into her scheme to save the Double-K. They'd played house— and slowly she had let herself believe the game was real.

Hell, to be totally honest, so had he.

Now he could see it coming. She had the marriage license and the baby she needed. But it wasn't going to be enough for her. He'd agreed to be temporarily roped. She wanted him tied and branded, as well.

But a lifetime arrangement wasn't the deal.

He stepped on the gas and pushed the speedometer needle over the speed limit. He had a plane to catch.

And his own heart to outrun.

In Nate's bedroom, Meggie hung up the phone feeling wounded and weepy. She sat on the edge of the bed for several minutes, her shoulders slumped, staring at the far wall. Then, with a soft, pitiful sigh, she got up and plodded out to the living room. She dropped into the jewel-green chair. She stared at an amethyst-centered geode on one of Nate's bookcases and allowed a grieved litany to play through her mind:

He promised before he left that he would be here. And now he suddenly has to fly off to Chicago. It's not fair. I've planned such a beautiful party. He could make a little effort. It's a special, special time. And he should be here. He should keep his promise and get home in time. Because I want him here. And he said before he left that he would be here....

About the third time through, she started to get sick of herself.

By the fifth time through, she'd had enough.

"I am being disgusting," she said to the amethyst-centered geode, since there was no one else to hear. "I am acting exactly like the clingy, demanding wife I swore I would never be." She stood. "I just better buck up."

The next morning, early, she knocked on Dolores's door. "Come on," she said, when the landlady opened the door.

"Where?"

"To the store. We have a lot of shopping to do."

Dolores beamed. "You know I adore to shop. Let me get *mi bolsa*." She disappeared down the hall and reappeared a moment later, clutching the big black patent-leather purse she carried with her whenever she went out. Then she called, "Benito, we are going shopping!"

From somewhere in the living room, Benny shouted, "Go! Have fun!"

"We will!"

They went to Dolores's favorite *carnicería* to pick up the turkey and the ham—and to Ralph's supermarket for most of the rest of the food. They visited a florist shop for fall leaves and autumn-colored flowers, with which Dolores planned to create twin centerpieces, one for each end of the two long pushed-together folding tables. They went to the party supply house, where they bought orange candles and adorable miniature turkeys and Indians and Pilgrims, which Dolores planned to include in her centerpieces.

They ate lunch out, at a little Mexican café Dolores liked. Of course the landlady insisted on treating. When they got home, in the late afternoon, they made pies. Mince and pecan and pumpkin and apple, rolling out the dough and filling the pie pans at Nate's, and using both their ovens for the baking.

Mrs. Tyrell came over for a few minutes while they were putting the pies together. They already had two in the oven.

"Oh, my, is that pecan pie I smell?" she asked.

"It is," Meggie answered. "Get yourself some coffee," Meggie said, "and have a seat."

Mrs. Tyrell helped herself and they talked for a few minutes of the party tomorrow. Mrs. Tyrell explained that she and her husband had been married only a few years. They had met as tenants of the same building, in the Valley. After their marriage, they had decided to move to West Hollywood when Mr. Tyrell found a part-time job with a recording company nearby.

"He likes to keep his hand in, you understand," Mrs. Tyrell said. "Once, he was a record producer. But that was years ago."

Dolores winked. "See? They are newlyweds, the same as you and Nate."

The sound of Nate's name sent a small surge of yearning through Meggie. She banished it with a nod and a grateful smile for Mrs. Tyrell. "I can't tell you how much we appreciate the loan of your beautiful things."

Mrs. Tyrell waved a perfectly manicured hand. "It will be lovely for me to see them put to use." She sighed, and for a moment she looked very sad. "Times change, don't they? But still, we cling to our mementos of the past."

Meggie wondered what Mrs. Tyrell meant by that exactly. But she didn't ask. It would have felt too much like prying. Each day, she learned a little more about Nate's neighbors. But friendship and trust weren't things a person could rush; they made their own time-tables.

Her stay here was temporary. Meggie had to remember that. She might or might not remain long enough to learn of Mrs. Tyrell's past.

Strange, she thought later, lying in Nate's bed alone, she felt so comfortable here. How quickly these two little Spanish-style apartment buildings in West Hollywood had become almost like home.

The next morning, Meggie and Dolores were up and cooking before the sun. All morning, the neighbors wandered in and out, bringing contributions to the feast or just stopping by for a few minutes to see how the preparations were getting along.

At nine, Benny took the van he and Dolores owned and drove over to the party store, which was open until noon that day so that customers could pick up any rental equipment they'd reserved. By ten-thirty, the two long tables extended from the kitchen halfway into the living room and Dolores had begun the intricate process of setting and decorating.

Meggie had just checked the turkey when Dolores asked her where the bag from the party store had gone.

"You know, the one with my little Indians and Pilgrims?"

"It's in the bedroom. I'll get it." Meggie headed down the hall.

As she passed the office, she heard Nate's business phone ring. She froze, her heart lurching in her chest. It could very well be Nate, calling from Chicago to check his messages.

Well, all right. It probably wasn't.

But it could be. And if she answered, she could wish him a Happy Thanksgiving. She could be upbeat and cheerful, show him that she'd gotten over her attack of the sulks the other day.

The phone rang for the third time. On the next ring, the machine would take it.

She shouldn't...

But she couldn't help herself. She shoved open the door and raced to the desk.

"Yes. Hello?" She remembered she probably ought to try to sound professional. "Um, this is Bravo Investigative Services, Megan speaking."

On the other end, there was nothing but silence. She wasn't sure how Nate's message-pickup device worked. Maybe it was all electronic, which would mean that if Nate were on the other end of the line, he would have no idea that she had answered instead of his machine.

"Hello?" she said, trying again.

She heard a cough, and then a throaty woman's voice asked hesitantly, "Is Nate Bravo there?"

It wasn't Nate. Disappointment made Meggie sigh.

And then she realized that she would have to take a message. She yanked open the center drawer of the desk in search of a pencil and paper.

"Are you there?" the woman asked.

Meggie found a pen and a yellow legal pad and shoved the drawer shut. "Yes, I'm here. But Mr. Bravo isn't."

A silence, then, "Oh. I see. Well. All right, then."

Meggie sensed that the woman meant to hang up. Nate would not be happy that she'd picked up his phone—and possibly cost him a job. She spoke briskly. "May I take a message?"

The woman let another silence elapse before admitting with reluctance, "It's...personal."

A girlfriend. Meggie just knew it. She wanted to scratch the woman's eyes out. She wanted to shout, "Stay away from my husband!" But then, she had no claim on Nate. Not really. And she had no right to try to frighten his girlfriends away.

And come to think of it, wouldn't a girlfriend call on the house line?

The woman said grimly, "I suppose, though, that I might as well leave a message. Would you wish him a happy Thanksgiving?"

"I'd be glad to. From who?"

"From his mother, Sharilyn."

Chapter Nine

"Hello? Are you still there?" asked Sharilyn.

Nate's mother. Meggie couldn't believe it. She'd never met the woman herself. People said Sharilyn had grown up in South Dakota somewhere. She and Bad Clint had met in Cheyenne and stayed there through the years of their marriage. Since Bad Clint and his father, Ross, never could stand each other, Clint refused to go near Medicine Creek or the Rising Sun.

But then, when Bad Clint died, Ross had convinced Sharilyn to let Nate live with him. And after that, Nate's mother had pretty much disappeared. To Meggie's recollection, Nate hadn't mentioned her since that first year he came to the Rising Sun—and then only to say how he hated her for making him live there.

"Hello?" Sharilyn asked again.

"Yes. Don't hang up. I'm still here. I'm just... surprised, that's all."

A wry laugh came over the line. "Didn't think Nate *had* a mother, did you?"

"Well, I—"

"It's all right. Just give him the message, okay? Goodbye."

"Wait."

A pause, then warily, "What?"

"I tried to make you think I was Nate's secretary. But I'm not really his secretary."

Sharilyn chuckled. "Yeah. I was onto you. I don't know a lot of secretaries who work on Thanksgiving."

"I'm...Nate's wife."

"Oh. I see."

Was she sad or happy to hear such news? Meggie hadn't a clue. "Everybody calls me 'Meggie.' I own a ranch not far from the Rising Sun, back in Wyoming."

"Well," Sharilyn said. And nothing else.

"Does Nate have a number where he can reach you?"

Sharilyn laughed, but there wasn't much humor in the sound. "He knows how to reach me. We...don't talk much. But we kind of keep tabs on each other."

"I understand," Meggie said. Though she didn't, not at all. Nate's Rolodex sat in the right-hand corner of the big, old desk. She pulled it close and flipped to the *B*s.

And there it was. First name only: Sharilyn. With a phone number. And a Los Angeles address.

"You live here," Meggie blurted out.

"What do you mean?"

"Here. You live here in L.A."

"So?"

"So...what are you doing this afternoon?"

"Excuse me?"

"It's Thanksgiving. Have you made plans for dinner?"

"Well, I—"

"Stop. I can tell by the way you said 'Well.' You're free."

A low sound escaped Sharilyn. "Free," she murmured, as if she didn't think much of the word.

"Well, are you? Are you free?"

"Yeah, all right. I'm free."

"Great. So that means you can come here, to Nate's. We're having a feast."

"A feast," Sharilyn repeated, sounding a little dazed.

"Yes. A big Thanksgiving Day feast. Most of the people in Nate's building will be coming. And some from next door."

"Oh, really, no. I couldn't."

"Yes, you could."

"Nate wouldn't—"

"Look. Don't worry about Nate. He'll be glad to see you, I'm sure." Meggie spoke with a good deal more confidence than she felt.

"But I—"

"And besides, to tell you the truth, I can't even be sure he'll be here for dinner. He had to fly to Chicago unexpectedly. He said he'd try to get back in time, but I don't know if he'll make it. So will you come?"

"I really—"

"Please, Sharilyn. Say you'll come."

Sharilyn said nothing.

Meggie added in a wheedling tone, "I would really like to meet you."

"You're...a very sweet girl."

"Great." Meggie spoke with finality. "You'll come."

Sharilyn let a lengthy silence elapse before conceding apprehensively, "All right. I will."

An hour later Meggie answered the door to find a tall, slim woman with black hair waiting on the other side.

Meggie smiled tentatively, thinking that the woman must once have been stunningly beautiful, though signs of a hard life showed in the lines that bracketed her mouth and fanned out from the corners of her dark, deep-set eyes. "Sharilyn?"

Sharilyn nodded. "And you're Meggie?"

"Yes."

The two women regarded each other. Meggie felt misty eyed. Here was Nate's mother, standing right in front of her. And for some crazy reason, she found herself thinking of her own mother, Mia, who had left her adoring husband and infant daughter behind to go in search of bright lights and good times.

Mia had found what she sought. She had died on a Manhattan street corner, run down by a reckless driver at dawn after a night spent club hopping and drinking fine champagne.

Always, in her most secret heart, Meggie had nurtured an impossible fantasy. That her mother hadn't really died. And that someday, Mia would come to see her. She would be beautiful, but a little sad, a little worn—a lot like Sharilyn, actually. She would have tears in her eyes. And she would say, "Whatever I did, wherever I went, I thought of you, Megan May. And I always, always loved you...."

Sharilyn arched a dark eyebrow. "Well?"

Meggie shook herself and stepped back. "Come on in." She led Sharilyn to the kitchen, where Dolores stood at the stove and Yolie worked at the sink, cleaning shrimp for the seafood cocktail that was Dolores's specialty.

"Welcome," Dolores said, beaming her wide, warm smile.

Sharilyn smiled back. "Thank you." She looked around anxiously.

"No está aquí," Dolores murmured gently.

Sharilyn frowned. "Excuse me?"

"Mr. Bravo. Your son. He is not here right now."

"Yes," Sharilyn replied in a mild voice. "I can see that."

Around one o'clock, the other guests began arriving. They would share an hour or two of cocktails, appetizers and good talk, then sit down for the huge meal.

After an initial nervous reserve, Sharilyn seemed to fit right in. And she and Peg knew each other.

"Sharilyn's the best damn waitress on Sunset Boulevard," Peg announced with great respect.

It turned out that Sharilyn worked as head waitress on the morning shift at a place called Dave's Café. Often, after a late night, Peg would drop in for breakfast before heading home. "Sharilyn takes care of her people," Peg said.

Sharilyn muttered a dry, "Thanks," and then swiftly changed the subject to the beauty of the table setting.

Meggie served appetizers, declined champagne with some regret and made sure everyone was comfortable. The talk ranged from football to Community Watch to the Christmas season and how it seemed to start earlier every year. Hector, who had most of his bandages off now, but still looked pretty gruesome at first glance, took an instant liking to Sharilyn. And she seemed friendly enough toward him. Meggie smiled at the two of them, sitting side by side on one of Nate's blue sofas, speaking in low, careful voices of the weather and their mutual love of musical theater. As she moved among her guests, Meggie tried not to let her mind stray to thoughts of Nate. She tried not to keep hoping that maybe, just maybe, he might still make it home before the end of the party....

After a miserable flight home, Nate picked up his car in the long-term parking lot at LAX. It was a quarter of two.

He had to have holes in his head. Nobody tried to get a last-minute flight out of O'Hare on Thanksgiving. It couldn't be done.

But Nate had done it—because he couldn't stop thinking about Meggie, and how hurt she'd sounded the last time he talked to her.

He felt like a jerk for copping out on her party—even if, once the party was over, he planned to get down to hard reality with her. He'd started thinking that if he could just make it in time for Thanksgiving dinner, then at least he could tell himself he hadn't stood her up for the big event.

His reasoning was stupid. Irrational. Nonsense. But he'd waited half the night anyway, for a chance at a flight. And then he'd lurched and bumped over the Rockies, listening to his flight mates toss their cookies as, from the cockpit, the pilot issued constant reassurances that this "minor turbulence" would pass.

Nate paid the excessive long-term parking fee and headed home. Once he got clear of the airport, the streets were relatively empty; most people would be in their houses, watching football and getting ready to pound down a little turkey and dressing.

He pulled into his carport space at two-thirty, got his bag from the trunk and headed for his front door. He was sticking his key in the lock, when the door swung back.

And there she was, her eyes shining, her dark hair with its gold and red lights curling softly around her flushed, happy face.

The warm air from inside came out and wrapped around him, scented of ham and roast bird, of cinnamon and cloves. He could hear laughter and voices from the other room.

"You made it," she said.

Something rose up inside him, something that ached and longed and scared the hell out of him. He dropped his bag inside the door and reached for her. She came into his arms, warm and soft, smelling of roses and Thanksgiving.

"Nate..." She breathed his name against his mouth.

He kissed her hard and long. Only a burst of laughter from the other room stopped him from swinging her up in his arms and carrying her down the hall to his bedroom.

She stepped back, her face pink, a tender smile on her lips. "Come on. We're just sitting down."

"Let me get rid of my bag."

"Sure."

She was still standing in the same place when he came back down the hall after dropping the duffel in the bedroom. And she looked a little flustered. "Nate, I...wanted to tell you..."

"What?"

"Well, we have an extra guest."

He had no idea what she was babbling about. "That's okay by me."

"Well. Good." Still, she looked undecided. And maybe a little bit guilty.

"What's going on?" he asked quietly.

"Happy Thanksgiving, Nate," said a familiar voice.

Nate looked over to see his mother standing in the doorway to the kitchen.

He was careful to treat the woman civilly. Meggie seated him next to her, a move he didn't appreciate at all. He passed the woman the gravy when she asked for it and tried not to look into her deep, sad eyes.

At the end of the meal, he turned to her. "I think you and I could use a few minutes. Alone."

Her eyes looked sadder than ever and her stiff shoulders seemed to droop. "All right."

As most of the others gravitated back toward the living room, Nate led Sharilyn down the hall and into his office.

"Have a seat." He gestured at the chair opposite his desk.

Sharilyn looked at the chair warily, then shook her head. "I think I might as well stand."

"Suit yourself." He shoved the door closed and moved into the room, leaving her standing uncomfortably by the door. When he got beyond his desk, he turned and looked at her, letting a beat or two elapse before he asked, "All right. What's going on?"

She put her hand against her heart. "I called. To wish you a Happy Thanksgiving. Meggie answered. She invited me to come over for dinner."

"And you came."

She lifted her chin and said nothing.

He demanded flatly, "Why?"

Her brows drew together in a pained expression. "Nate, I just want—"

"What? You want what?"

"Some kind of…understanding, between us."

"We understand each other. Perfectly."

"Oh, Nate, that's not true. You know it's not."

"Do you need money?"

"No. It's not money. You know that."

"Do I?"

"Please, Nate…"

He let out a long, bored breath of air. "You shouldn't have come here. And I think you know that."

"I only wanted—"

He waved a hand to cut off her pointless explanations. "If you're short of cash, I'll help you out. Otherwise, I've got nothing to say to you." With that, he turned away from her, toward the window. As usual, the green blind was halfway up. He looked across the next-door neighbors' driveway at the hibiscus bush—a little scraggly this time of year—that grew against the building there. The shadows were lengthening. It would be dark soon.

"Nate…" Sharilyn said, trying again.

He refused to turn or to say a word.

She murmured sadly, "All right, then."

He resolutely continued staring out the window, ignoring her. After a moment, he heard the sound of the door opening and her footsteps on the hardwood floor, moving out into the hall. He waited another few seconds, to be sure she had really gone. Then he turned and followed after her.

In the living room, Sharilyn headed straight for Meggie. Nate stood in the hall entry, watching her make her goodbyes.

"Thank you so much for a great meal. But I'm afraid I've got to get going now."

Meggie frowned. "But, Sharilyn, there's still dessert."

"No. I really have to go."

Meggie tried teasing. "Sharilyn. These are incredible pies. My grandma Kane's secret recipes. People have fought their way through blizzards for pies like these."

"Thanks. Really." Sharilyn was backing toward the door. "Nice to meet you all." She glanced around, a wooden smile stretching her mouth.

Meggie looked up then and right at Nate. Her eyes accused him. He stared back at her, meeting her glare with one of his own. When Sharilyn reached him and went on past, he followed her to the door, watched her go out and closed it behind her.

Then he joined the party, where everyone seemed to be having a great time. He poured himself a glass of champagne. And then, refusing to let himself be snared by Meggie's reproachful glances, he went and sat by the old guy from next door, Leverson, who still looked like a refugee from a horror movie, but claimed he was feeling better every day.

"Call me 'Hector,' why don't you?" Leverson suggested. Then he added rather dreamily, "Your mother is a lovely, charming woman. It's a shame she had to leave so soon."

Nate made a low noise in his throat that Hector could interpret any way he chose, and then got up to pour himself more champagne. He figured he was going to need a river of the stuff before the evening finally came to an end.

* * *

Three hours later, most of the guests had said goodbye, all smiling and laughing and swearing they'd had a terrific time.

Mrs. Tyrell suggested, "We'll have to do it again next year."

Meggie smiled and made a noncommittal noise in response. Next year, she wouldn't be here. But now was hardly the time to mention that fact. She glanced over to find Nate watching her. She looked away. She had a few things to say to him—later, when they were alone.

The Garnicas lingered to help clean up. Dolores and Yolie worked with Meggie washing dishes, while Benny and Nate lugged the tables, chairs and linens down to the Garnicas' van so they'd be ready to go back to the rental shop the next morning.

As soon as all of the Tyrells' treasured china sparkled like new, they toted it across the landing, where Mrs. Tyrell put it away. Then Meggie and Dolores packed up two-thirds of the leftovers for the Garnicas to enjoy.

Finally, at a little after nine o'clock, the Garnicas departed. Meggie stood at the top of the landing and watched them bustle down the stairs, laden with their booty of pies, candied yams and turkey—and a generous portion of spiral-cut ham.

When she turned back to the apartment, Nate was leaning in the doorway, watching her.

They shared a long, telling look. And then Meggie tried to move past him.

He shifted in the doorway to block her path.

She made a low noise. "Come on, Nate."

He shook his head, the action slow and insolent. He'd been drinking champagne steadily since he'd thrown his mother out. It hadn't seemed to affect him during the party, but now the signs of one too many were starting to show. His eyes were heavy lidded and his full mouth looked just a little bit mean.

Meggie understood his desire to dull the pain that his own actions must have caused him. But she didn't approve—either of the way he'd treated Sharilyn, or of drinking too much as a solution to anything. She'd thought they would talk over what he'd done. But now that she realized his condition, she only wanted to get away from him until he'd had time to sober up.

"Nate. Move."

"Meggie May." He said her name with great solemnity.

"Just move. Please."

His bloodshot eyes bored through her. But then, with a lazy shrug of his big shoulders, he let her pass.

She went straight down the hall to the bathroom, where she intended to take a long, soothing bath. Unfortunately, Nate followed after her and slid in front of the door when she tried to swing it shut.

"Get out of the way, Nate."

He didn't move, only crossed his arms insolently over his broad chest and leaned his head back against the door. "What is your problem?" he asked the ceiling, in a tone of infinite weariness.

"You. You keep blocking my way. Move."

He lowered his head and looked at her. "No."

With some regret, she gave up the idea of that nice, tension-relieving bath. "Fine." She turned on her heel and started back down the hall.

She got about three steps before he grabbed her arm. Meggie froze in midstride. "Let go of me."

"We have to talk."

She turned on him then, her lip curling in a sneer. "I don't want to talk to you now. You're drunk."

He wiggled a finger at her. "No. Incorrect. I am not drunk. I am...slightly numb."

"Right."

"But not numb enough." He pronounced each word with great care, as if he feared his own tongue might trip him up.

"Just let go of me, Nate."

"Meggie—"

"Let go."

He closed his eyes. "Meggie..." The word held utter exhaustion.

Her heart turned over then and her anger at him melted away. He looked so tired, and so bewildered. Gently, she laid her hand over his and peeled the fingers away from her arm.

"Come on." She eased around him and started pulling him toward the bedroom. "Sleep it off. We can talk in the morning." Surprisingly, he followed after her, obedient as a child.

In the bedroom, she sat him down on the bed. Then, kneeling, she pulled off his boots. He stuck out one foot and then the other for her, murmuring "Meggie, Meggie, Meggie," making a weary litany of her name.

When she had the boots off, she rose and took his shoulders, guiding him onto his back. He stretched out with sigh, his eyes already closed. She took the spare quilt from the top shelf of the closet and settled it over him.

"Meggie..." he whispered, already asleep.

She kissed him on the forehead and then tiptoed to the door. She would have that long bath after all, and then she'd slide under the quilt beside him and get some rest herself.

Tomorrow, she'd let him sleep late. And then, after

she poured a few cups of coffee down him, she'd tell him just what she thought of the way he'd behaved with Sharilyn.

But it didn't work out quite as Meggie planned.

She woke around three to a feeling of loneliness. She sat up in bed. "Nate?" No answer came. His side of the bed was empty.

Worried, and telling herself not to be, Meggie pushed back the blanket, pulled on the robe she'd borrowed from Nate and padded out to the hall.

Past the front door, a wedge of light spilled from the kitchen onto the hardwood floor. The smell of freshly brewed coffee scented the air. Meggie pulled Nate's robe closer around her and moved toward the light.

She found Nate sitting at the kitchen table, staring into a coffee mug. "Nate. Are you all right?"

He looked up. His eyes were still red, but piercingly alert. He picked up the mug and drained the contents. "I'm fine." He stood and carried the mug to the counter, where he refilled it. Then he held the pot toward her. "Coffee?"

She shook her head.

He lifted an eyebrow at her, smirking a little. "How surprising."

She frowned. "What does that mean?"

He waved a hand, dismissing both her question and his own remark. Then he shoved the pot back on the warmer and returned to the table, where he dropped into his chair again and gestured at the seat across from him.

"Come on," he said. "Sit down. Time to talk."

She did want to discuss the way he'd behaved with Sharilyn. But there had to be a better time to do it.

"Nate, it's three in the morning. I really think we might as well let this wait until—"

He leveled a hard stare at her. "Look. I'm stone sober now. And it's time we hashed this out."

Reluctantly, she murmured, "Fine."

"Sit down, then."

She marched to the table and plunked herself into the chair across from him.

For a moment, once she was seated, he stared at her—a totally unreadable kind of look. Then he brought the full mug to his lips and took a careful sip.

She assumed he must be waiting for her to begin. So she plunged right in. "You were really rotten to your mother."

He winced at her accusation and must have burned his mouth. He swore and set the mug down, hard enough that coffee slopped over the rim. "I wouldn't have been rotten to her," he said silkily, "if she hadn't been here. But *somebody* invited her here. Who was that, do you think?"

"You know who."

"Say it."

"Me."

He faked a surprised look, one that scraped her nerves raw. "Oh, really? You? What a revelation."

She kept her head high. "And I'm glad that I did it."

"I can see that."

Meggie breathed deeply, trying to keep her anger leashed. She felt that he was totally in the wrong about this—and making it worse by taunting her. "Nate. She called on your *business line*. Your business line. She doesn't even have your private number, does she?"

"No, she doesn't."

Meggie's disbelief wouldn't be contained. "She lives

right here. In L.A. I didn't even know that. You never said a word."

He made a harsh sound. "So?"

"So, we could have had her over. We could have spent a little time with her. We could have—"

He raised himself halfway out of his chair, put both hands on the table and leaned across at her. "You refuse to get the picture here," he said in a furious whisper. "I don't want her over. I don't want anything to do with her."

Meggie met his attack with quiet dignity. "That's cruel."

He snorted. "Life's cruel."

"If you would only—"

He dropped back into his chair and slapped a hand on the table. "Stop. You don't know what you're talking about. You don't get this situation at all. So let it be."

"No, Nate. It isn't right. She's your mother. And I think she really loves you. All she wants is a chance to—"

"Listen to me, Meggie. *I* want you to leave this alone."

"No. It's not right. You won't even give her a chance. I know you feel she abandoned you, after your dad died. But everything worked out all right, didn't it? You had a much better life with your grandfather and your cousins than you ever would have had with Sharilyn."

"You don't know a damn thing about the life I would have had with her if my grandfather hadn't butted in."

"I think I do know. I think Sharilyn did what she thought was best for you. She was a woman alone, and you weren't exactly an easy kid to handle. And she knew that your grandfather would take you in hand and—''

''Stop.''

''No. Listen. She knew that your grandfather would be able to deal with you.''

''That's garbage, Meggie May. Sentimental garbage.''

''No, it's not. She wanted—''

''You don't know her. You don't know what the hell she wanted.'' His red-rimmed eyes gleamed brightly now, with anger. And something else. Something deep and old and ugly with hurt.

''Oh, Nate...'' Involuntarily, she reached across and touched his hand.

He jerked back as if she'd burned him. ''Don't.''

''Nate, please—''

''No. Back off.''

''If you'll only give her a chance.''

''Forget it. She'll get no chance from me.''

''But why not?''

''You don't need to know.''

''I do. Please. Tell me. Let me understand.''

He looked out the window, at the lights of L.A. beyond the carport, and then back at her. ''You just have to keep pushing.''

''I really want to understand.''

''Fine. All right. The damn woman *sold* me.''

Meggie frowned. ''Sold you?''

''When I was fourteen years old, she sold me to my grandfather.''

''Sold you—for money?''

Nate looked at her squarely; now his eyes were flat black stones. ''Yeah, for money.''

''But how—''

"When my father died, my grandfather offered my mother fifteen thousand dollars if she would give me up."

"No..."

"Yeah." He looked out the window again, at the darkness and the tiny lights that went on and on, up onto the surrounding hills and all the way to the horizon line.

"But how do you know that?"

"I overheard him make her the offer."

"Overheard?"

"Right." Nate rubbed a hand down his face. "My mother thought I was out running wild when she had her little talk with him. But I came in through the back. And I listened in. I heard my grandfather say a lot of nasty things about my father—what a loser he was, what a disgrace to the Bravo name." Nate made a low, scoffing sound. "Everything he said was true, of course. But all the same, I hated him for saying it, for being so damn smug about it. He talked a lot about how he knew it was partly his fault, the way my father had turned out. That he'd been too tough at the wrong times—and not loving enough in general. He told my mother he wanted to make sure I had a chance to be the man my father wasn't. And that she'd be doing me a favor to take the money and disappear."

"What did she say to all that?"

"Not a damn thing. He did all the talking. Finally, when he'd said it all, he told her he'd come back the next day for her answer. Then he left."

"What did you do then?"

"I came out of my hiding place. I begged her not to do it. I said we could make it, together, that we could get by. Maybe we didn't have the kind of life other people thought was a good life. But it was *our* life. I thought it mattered. I thought we had each other and that that was the bottom line.''

A small, sympathetic sound escaped Meggie.

Nate shot her a hard glance, then turned away again. ''Don't look at me like that. It was years ago. And you're right. I did well enough at the ranch, in the end. But I'm not giving an inch when it comes to that woman. She took the money and sent me away. She *said* it was the best thing for me. But that was just an excuse she made so that she could get rid of me—so that she could be free.''

Meggie watched him as he stared on at the lights beyond the window. She ached for the boy he'd been—and she understood at last why he'd grown so angry every time she tried to give him money in return for all he'd agreed to do for her. What she couldn't understand was why he wouldn't let go of his anger at Sharilyn. It had been so many years, after all. Certainly time enough to get beyond the hurt. And Sharilyn so clearly wanted to reach out to him. What ever kind of mother she had been years ago, anyone could see she was a kind, thoughtful person now. Why not make peace with her? What harm could that possibly do?

Nate looked down into his empty mug and then up into Meggie's eyes. ''So that's that. She wanted to be free. And she *is* free. And I don't want a damn thing to do with her.''

''Oh, Nate, I still really believe that—''

''Look. It doesn't matter what you believe. She wanted freedom, and she's got it. And I understand her. Because I'm just like her.''

''But you *don't* understand her. Not really. You're just getting even with her, that's all. You're just nursing a grudge—hurting her and yourself, too—because you felt abandoned when she gave you up. Have you ever thought that it's just possible she really did do it for your own good? It's just possible it hurt her to lose you as much as it hurt you to be sent away. You should—''

"Meggie." His voice was as hard as his eyes.

"What?"

"I don't need anyone telling me what I *should* do."

"But I—"

"This is my damn life. You've got no right to tell me how I ought to live it. Am I making myself clear here?"

Meggie stared into his cold, remote face. And it occurred to her that she'd got herself into a losing battle here, one that had only ended up making him angry at her.

"Am I making myself clear?"

She sighed. "Yes. All right."

"All right, what?"

She spoke with measured calm. "You've made yourself clear."

"Good." He lifted his mug from the table and set it away from him, in a gesture of finality. "And now that we've wrapped up the subject of Sharilyn, let's finish up the rest of this mess."

She frowned at him, not understanding. "Finish up?"

"Meggie, let's stop playing games."

"Games?"

He shook his head. "You've been keeping something from me, for a while now. Haven't you?"

Reality started to dawn. "Well, I—"

"A pretty important little piece of information."

Her heart thudded to a stop, then started thundering. "Nate, let's not—"

"We've been having such a great time, playing house."

She opened her mouth, but no words came out.

He prodded. "Haven't we?"

She closed her eyes.

"Haven't we?"

"Yes. All right."

"All right, what?"

She gave him the words he'd demanded to hear. "We've been having a great time."

"But there *was* a goal. Wasn't there?"

She only stared at him.

"Wasn't there?"

"Nate, please—"

"Just give me an answer."

"Yes. All right. Fine. A goal, yes."

"And what was the goal, Meggie?"

"Stop it."

"Meggie. What was the goal?"

She looked out the window. "For me to get pregnant."

"What was that? Speak up."

"You can be so cruel."

"The goal, Meggie. Name me the goal."

She faced him. "That's enough."

"Then just tell me. Have we reached the goal here?"

She sat very straight.

"Have we, Meggie?"

She made her tone as cold as his. "Yes, Nate. We have."

"Fine, then. You've got everything you needed from me. And it's time you went on home."

Chapter Ten

Nate started calling the airlines right then, at three-thirty in the morning. He wanted her out of his hair ASAP. But it was Thanksgiving weekend. After an hour of calling, he found nothing available—unless she wanted to try standby—until Monday morning. He reserved a seat on the Monday flight.

He looked at Meggie with grim expectation when he gave her the information. She knew he was waiting for her to volunteer to go and sit at the airport. She didn't volunteer. Monday was three days away. A lot could happen in three days.

She had no right to hope he might change his mind, and she knew it. Yet hope burned like an eternal flame within her. She had promised herself not to try to hold him. But now that the moment to let him go had come, she refused to rush toward it. She would take the flight on Monday. But until then, he could just put up with her.

Which was exactly what he did: he put up with her. He slept on the couch Friday night and he spoke to her only when necessary. He waited for her to get on that plane and get out of his life.

Saturday afternoon, while Nate was out doing heaven knew what, Dolores knocked on the door. One look at Meggie's face and Dolores demanded, "Okay, what did that man do to you?"

Meggie ushered her in and gave her coffee and pumpkin pie and told her everything.

After calling Nate several shocking names in Spanish, Dolores told Meggie, "Still, we must remember, that man is wild and crazy for you. He cannot keep his hands off of you. And sometimes, when he looks at you..." Dolores made a show of fanning herself. Then she winked at Meggie. "Maybe you will just have to drive him mad with desire, eh? So he cannot let you go."

Meggie shook her head. "Dolores, he slept on the couch last night. He's very careful not to give me a chance to drive him mad with desire."

Dolores muttered more imprecations in Spanish. Then she brightened a little. "Ah well, at least there will be a little one. A woman needs her babies. A baby is life. And who can say? You do have a little time, to tempt him, before you go. And that baby will always be there, something you both share for all eternity."

Meggie sighed, not particularly heartened. "I guess so."

That evening, Nate didn't come home. Meggie made turkey noodle soup and ate alone, hardly tasting the food, staring out the window, longing for him and calling herself a fool.

She went to bed at ten, then tossed and turned for hours. Finally, sometime after two, she drifted into a fitful sleep.

When she got up in the morning, she found Nate sleeping on the couch. They sat down to breakfast together. He read the *Times* as he ate. When he was finished, he rinsed his dishes and stuck them in the dishwasher.

"I've got to go away overnight," he said.

She looked up from her half-empty plate. "Liar."

He shrugged. "I'll be back tomorrow, in time to take you to LAX."

"Don't bother. I can take a taxi."

"I said I'd be here in time. I will."

She couldn't stop herself from giving it one more try. "Nate, if you'll only—"

"We had an agreement. You have what you needed. Now let it go."

At that moment, hope finally left her. It drained from her, leaving her empty. And sad. She looked out at the parking lot and the carports. "All right. See you tomorrow, then."

He went back to the bedroom—she supposed to pack an overnight bag. A few minutes later, she heard the front door close. She watched him, when he appeared at the carports, tossing his bag behind the seat, pulling his black car out. And driving away.

Mrs. Tyrell knocked on Meggie's door that afternoon. "I hear you're leaving us."

Meggie gave her neighbor a rueful smiled. "Dolores has been talking."

Mrs. Tyrell laughed, a low, velvety sound. "Everybody in both buildings knows. And we will miss you."

Meggie stepped back. "Will you come in? I could use a little company."

Mrs. Tyrell nodded.

Meggie asked, "Coffee?"

"How about tea, for a change?"

Meggie brewed a pot of herbal tea and they sat at the table, sipping.

"My mother always drank tea," Mrs. Tyrell said musingly. "She felt coffee was for barbarians."

Meggie asked, "Were you raised here, in L.A.?"

"Oh, no. I'm from Philadelphia. And I lied about Terence."

Meggie didn't know anyone by that name. "Terence?"

"My husband."

"Oh." Meggie stared across the table at her neighbor, recognizing the moment when an acquaintance becomes a friend. "I didn't know your husband's first name."

"Now you do. And I'm Lurline."

"It's pretty."

"My mama chose it. And I didn't meet Terence at the apartment in the Valley."

"You didn't?"

Lurline shook her head. "I found him again there, almost thirty years later. But I met him when I was eighteen years old."

"In Philadelphia?"

"Um-hm. I loved him the moment I saw him."

Meggie instantly thought of Nate. "Oh, I know how that is. What happened?"

"My mama didn't approve of him."

"Oh, no."

"Oh, yes. 'A wild boy in a cheap suit,' she called him. She forbade me to see him. And I always did what Mama said."

"You turned him away."

"I did. He went to New York. And then came here. Had his big, fancy career in the record industry. He married three times, before I came to get him."

"Three times?"

Lurline smiled. "He has five children. I adore them all."

"And what about you?"

"I never married," Lurline said. "Until I found my Terence again." She leaned closer to Meggie. "That was after Mama died, of course." Lurline laughed her velvety laugh.

"You went looking for him when your mother died?"

"Yes, I did. When Mama died, I sold her house and packed up most of her fine, old things and moved out West—all the way to the San Fernando Valley."

"You knew where to find him?"

Lurline nodded. "That was my one rebellion against Mama in all those years. I kept track of my Terence."

"You wrote to him?"

"Never." Lurline's full lips were pursed in disapproval. "He was a married man. Most of the time."

"But how—"

"I had ways."

"So. You found him and married him."

"That's right. So never say that love is over. It might

just be waiting. Sometimes it waits for years and years.''

"I'll try to remember that."

"Yes. Do."

Meggie cast Lurline a hesitant look.

"Go ahead," Lurline said. "Ask."

"All right. Did all of your fine things once belong to your mother?"

"Yes." Lurline sighed. "Sometimes, quite frankly, I feel as if *they* own *me*. Especially all that mahogany furniture. The scale is so wrong for our apartment. What I wouldn't give for a little bleached oak here and there."

Meggie laughed. "So sell some of it."

"Oh, I couldn't. Terence wouldn't let me."

Meggie blinked in surprise. "Why not?"

Lurline's smile grew secretive. "Oh, I shouldn't say."

"You should. Come on."

"He gets such...pleasure from it all."

"From your mother's things?"

"Yes. He says every time he sits at her table, eats off her dishes—or sleeps in her bed, he has the satisfaction of knowing that the wild boy in the cheap suit got Mama's precious daughter after all." Now Lurline looked pensive. "But maybe someday the thrill will wear off. Don't you think?"

"Who can say?"

"Oh, Meggie, you are so right. Who can say? When it comes to a man, who can ever say?"

Meggie spent another night alone. Nate showed up as promised, early the next morning, in time to drive her to the airport.

The sun shone down bright and cheerful when they went out to get in the car.

The Garnicas, Hector Leverson, Edie and Peg all came out to tell her goodbye. Dolores grabbed Meggie and burst into tears. And Hector told her he would never forget her.

Edie said, "I will miss our little strolls, dear."

Peg added, "Don't stay away forever. Come back and see us sometime."

And Nate just stood there, waiting for his neighbors to go back to their apartments so he could take Meggie to the airport and be free of her.

Strange. Meggie had told herself during the whole of their brief time together that she knew it was destined to end. She had convinced herself that she believed it.

But she hadn't believed it, not really.

Deep in her heart, she'd been sure that Nate would see the light. That the happiness they'd shared would finally convince him he should spend his life at her side.

It hadn't worked out that way. Instead, he had given her exactly what she'd asked of him.

And no more.

Chapter Eleven

Meggie arrived at the small airport in Sheridan late that afternoon. Farrah was waiting to take her the rest of the way home. Both six-year-old Kate and little Davey had come, too.

Meggie was relieved to see the children. Because of them, she wouldn't have to answer any uncomfortable questions during the drive to the ranch. The questions would come later, of course. But Meggie told herself she'd be better able to deal with them then. And if both Farrah and Sonny were there when they talked, then Meggie would only have to tell the sad story once.

Meggie spent most of the drive staring silently out the window at the miles and miles of pastureland, now cloaked in a glaring mantle of stark white. The cottonwoods in the creek bottoms were stripped bare, sticking up their naked branches toward the steel-gray sky.

* * *

That night, Farrah and Sonny insisted that Meggie have dinner at the bunkhouse.

As soon as the kids were in bed, they sat her down and asked what was going on. Fed up with lies and half-truths, Meggie told them everything.

"So he never meant to stay with you," Sonny declared indignantly when she was through. "He planned all along to walk away as soon as he got you pregnant."

Meggie sighed. "Sonny. It was what I asked him to do. What I *needed* him to do. Or we would have lost the Double-K."

Sonny shook his head. "You're a good-looking woman, with a big heart and a working ranch. You've had offers—I know you have. You could have found yourself a real husband. Someone who would have stood by you."

"I didn't want just *someone*. I only wanted Nate. And for a little while, I had him." She put her hand on her stomach cherishingly. "And there *will* be a baby. Nate's baby. It's not everything I dreamed of. But it's a lot closer than I ever thought I was going to get."

Sonny and Farrah exchanged baffled glances.

Meggie smiled. "I know you don't understand. And that's okay. I just want you to know that I am fine. That we're going to keep the Double-K. That in the spring, you'll have a new niece or nephew. I hope that you'll help me to raise him—or her—right."

Of course they promised that they would.

A bit later, Meggie returned to her own house. In spite of her exhaustion after the long flight home, she stayed awake late. She missed Nate's warmth beside her. And the wind was up, beating around the eaves, making a haunted, crying, lonely sound.

The next morning, born rancher that she was, Meggie

rose in the dark. She made a fire and drank her tea and watched the winter sun lift its face slowly to light the new day.

A week later, Meggie received her first letter from Dolores. It read: "Your husband is gone. Off on one of those jobs of his. And when he his here, I do not talk to him. I give him looks like dirt. Did you know that my own grandmother was a *bruja*, a woman of magic? Maybe I will do something ugly, with chickens. He will suffer. And then he will beg you to return to him...."

Meggie shot a letter back, commanding Dolores to do no such thing.

Dolores replied that she had only been joking. She was a modern Catholic woman, after all, and not superstitious in the least.

After that, the letters went back and forth. Meggie tried to write once a week and Dolores did the same. Meggie loved reading all the gossip, how Edie's son had tried to make her move to a rest home, but Edie had steadfastly refused.

Community Watch was still going strong. "We meet every two weeks," Dolores wrote. "I usually make the cookies. No one is attacking us, so I think we must be doing the job right. And I learned some hot gossip. Mr. Hector Leverson goes very often to a café on Sunset. You know the one I mean. It is called Dave's and we both know who is the head waitress there...."

Christmas came and went. Meggie, Sonny, Farrah and the kids spent it together. On the Sunday before New Year's, Meggie saw Cash and Abby at church in town.

Abby took Meggie aside and spoke frankly, as Abby tended to do. "You're pregnant, aren't you?"

"Am I getting that big?"

"Well, it does show. But you look good— Oh, Meggie. I'm so sorry."

"Don't be. I want this baby."

"I don't mean about the baby. You know what I mean. Nate." Abby groaned. "He is hopeless. Worse than Cash was, I think. And Cash was pretty bad, let me tell you. He ran away from happiness as fast as he could. You don't want to know what I went through with him. I'll spare you the details, but it was bad. Very bad. And Nate's a lot like Cash, really. Oh, I know. Nate's got that bad-boy thing going. And Cash was always everyone's knight in shining armor. But I mean, Cash lost his mother when he was twelve. And Nate lost his father when he was fourteen. And both of them ended up pretty much orphans, since the parent they had left dumped them off at the ranch. So my theory is, they're both terrified to love." Abby laughed. "You're looking kind of cross-eyed, Meggie. I'm talking too much, huh?" She frowned. "But all kidding aside, Nate didn't even come home for Christmas this year. That's a bad sign. He always comes home for that, at least. To tell you the truth, we're all a little worried."

Meggie offered the reassurance Abby seemed to be seeking. "He's all right. I keep in touch with his landlady. She says he's working a lot, but he's fine."

"Well. Good. I guess. Oh, Meggie. I know he loves you. He's always loved you."

"He wants his freedom."

"He is a complete fool."

Before they said goodbye, Meggie remembered to congratulate Abby on her recent graduation, with honors, from the University of Colorado.

Abby smiled her thanks and then told Meggie that

Tess DeMarley's mother had died. Tess was housemate to Abby's mother, Edna. "Poor Tess. She had to spend her Christmas in Rapid City, taking care of all the funeral arrangements."

Meggie made a mental note to send Tess a condolence card.

"But the good news," Abby said, "is that Zach finally asked Tess out."

Meggie smiled at that. Everyone in town knew that Zach Bravo had had his eye on the pretty widow who looked after Abby's mother. They'd all been waiting for him to make his move. And now, at last, he had.

"They'll end up married—just you wait," Abby predicted.

Meggie saw no reason to disagree.

In the first weeks of the new year, Meggie spent her days getting feed to the stock and her nights trying not to give in to depression. She did pretty well, actually. The baby helped. When things seemed loneliest, she would put her hand on her growing stomach and think loving thoughts of the life she would share with her new little one. Soon enough, she would find herself smiling, feeling that things weren't so bad after all.

Dolores wrote faithfully, alternately praising her grandchildren and complaining about them, reporting all the news from her two apartment buildings. In every letter, she made some mention of Nate:

He is doing fine, that man of yours. As fine as he deserves to do, staying all alone and acting like he hates the world....

Yesterday, he came down to pay the rent. He tried to stick the money where the mail goes. But

I am watching for him. I pull open the door and give him a big, mean smile. "Good morning, Mr. Bravo," I say to him. "And how are you doing lately?" He coughs and looks very scared. He should be scared. I am thinking bad thoughts about him. "I'm just fine, Dolores," he tells me. And then he sticks out the check. "Here. The rent." "Thank you, Mr. Bravo," I say, so polite. He turns to go and I say to his back, so sweet I know it makes shivers down his spine, "You take good care of yourself now."

Meggie, I can promise you. A little chicken blood and a few words of power and that man will come running to your side. Just kidding. Ha-ha....

January faded into February. Meggie was six months pregnant and serious winter feeding of the stock was well under way. Mostly, Meggie drove the vehicles, leaving the heavy lifting to Sonny as much as she could. Dr. Pruitt, who ran the clinic in town, warned Meggie to start thinking about the baby more.

"You're coming to the point where you'll just have to back off a little," he said.

"Come on, Doc. It's almost calving time."

"Hire an extra man or two. And talk to Farrah. Maybe you'll have to take over some of the work close to home and let her go out with Sonny to look after the herd."

That night, Meggie sat down with her cousin and his wife. She laid out the doctor's orders. Farrah declared that she'd do her best to fill Meggie's boots, even though she'd never be the rancher Meggie was. They decided that when calving time came, Meggie would handle the cooking for everyone and look after the kids. Farrah would take over Meggie's work as best she could and Sonny would work even harder than usual, to pick up the slack.

Meggie put out the word that she could use an extra hand, but it was the dead of winter and cowboying didn't pay much. She just hoped someone worth hiring would show up in the next month or two.

On the fifteenth of February, Edna Heller and Tess DeMarley threw Meggie a surprise baby shower at Edna's house in town. Abby came, too, of course, and so did Farrah, plus a couple of women Meggie had known since her school days. They played silly games and ate cake and punch.

Edna clucked over Meggie constantly through the party, asking her if she was feeling all right, fetching her pillows to support her back—and muttering complaints about Nate under her breath.

Meggie opened the brightly wrapped packages to find a full layette from Edna, a set of receiving blankets from Tess and a windup swing from Abby. Sonny had already made her a changing table, but still there was a gift from Farrah, too.

"You shouldn't have," Meggie told her cousin's wife.

"Oh, yes, I should."

Inside the box was a handmade quilt, mittens and a hat. "Oh, Farrah. They're beautiful."

Farrah smiled in pleasure at Meggie's obvious delight in her gift.

When she got home, Meggie took the new things up to the room next to her own, which she'd been fixing up for the baby over the last few weeks. Meggie put the tiny shirts and soft rompers away in the bureau, struck with wonder at the thought that in a few months, her baby would be wearing them.

The cold, dreary days went by. Meggie still went out with Sonny. But the time drew steadily nearer when she would have to switch places with Farrah and do a ranch wife's work—not an easy job, by any means. But at least Farrah's work didn't include things like pulling cows from frozen streams. Even driving the pickup was something Meggie would have to give up soon; her stomach was starting to get in the way of the wheel.

Meggie did worry that when calving time came, they'd have more work to do than hands to do it; yet still, a kind of peace had settled over her. A fullness. An acceptance. That she and her family would get by, one way or another. That her baby would be born and life would go on.

She looked for beauty where she could find it. And even on the dreariest days, beauty managed to find her.

One freezing evening at the very end of February, Meggie came in alone at dark. Sonny had knocked off early and taken Farrah and the kids into Buffalo for a visit with Farrah's mom, who ran a motel there.

As Meggie climbed from the pickup, seven hungry heifers bawled at her from the corral. They were close to their calving time, well ahead of the rest of the herd. Meggie and Sonny had put them in the corral so they could keep a close eye on them. Meggie grinned at the sound of them. She felt a real affinity with them lately; like them, she was big and ungainly and getting close to her time.

Crusted snow crunched under her boots as she tossed the heifers hay and grain cake, a process that took her much longer than it used to. Her back ached a little and her growing stomach slowed her down. Plus, she tried to be careful not to hurt herself or the baby whenever she attempted heavy work.

When the heifers had their feed, Meggie leaned on the corral rail for a minute, watching, listening to them crunch on the cake, feeling the cold down to her bones, but feeling kind of peaceful, too. The sky overhead was studded with stars—stars that always looked so much brighter, somehow, in the winter.

The chinook, a warm southern wind, came up as Meggie leaned there watching the heifers. It blew in the way it always did, seemingly from nowhere, to warm the winter world. Meggie sighed and smiled. She closed her eyes and let the warmth whip at her, swirling around her, feeling the temperature rise and the winter cold retreat.

The melting snow had started dripping from the eaves and cutting tiny rivulets in the blanket of white on the ground by the time she went inside. Meggie ate and got ready for bed smiling, as the chinook blew around the house, rattling the windows and making the roof creak.

She dreamed of a night, years and years ago, when she'd stood in the yard and, like tonight, a chinook had blown in, wild and warm, to thaw the frozen world of winter. That night Meggie had seen the aurora borealis: the fabulous many-colored northern lights. The chinook had whipped around her, pulling at her jacket and playing with her hair, and the great pipes of shimmering color had come alive in the north sky, long, leaping tubes of light, jumping high and fading down, waterfalls of pure color, dancing against the darkness of the night.

In her dream, Meggie lived it all again. And it seemed as if the rising towers of colored light were blown by the warm wind, pushed higher by the gusts of the chinook.

In her dream, she tipped her head to the sky, smiling. And she felt a hand slide into her own. She whispered, "Nate," and heard him gently answer, "Meggie."

And she woke, suddenly, alone in the bed that had been her father's.

Outside, the wind still blew. And the sound of Nate's voice was in it, warm and tender and full of all the promises she had longed for that he would never make to her. She rested her hand on the pregnant swell of her belly, turned her head and closed her eyes, hoping to slip back into the same dream.

But Nate and the dream of the northern lights had faded to memory. Only the roundness beneath her hand, the promise of the life he'd given into her care, remained.

By the next morning, the chinook had blown itself out. The deep, hard snow of the night before had melted down to patches on the wet, cold ground. A blizzard moved in that night, turning the world into a blur of flying white. By the time the blizzard moved on, the snow lay thick and white on the land once more.

In the first weeks of March, the heifers started to calve. Meggie had no choice by then but to stay close to the house, cooking and watching the kids and hand-feeding any calves too premature or ill to suck. The heifers they'd worried about, the ones they'd kept in the corral, had dropped their calves and been let out to pasture by the second week of March.

By the third week of March, the older cows started to calve. A good portion of the Double-K became one huge maternity ward. Sonny and Farrah were out every morning before dawn, trying to keep track of births that ranged over several thousand acres, to get to any cows that were having trouble, to help any calves that had gotten separated from their mothers in the spring storms that blew across the prairie, full of cold, blinding fury, driving the cows before the wind.

If possible, they brought the problems home to Meggie in the bed of a pickup, or even slung over the front of a saddle. She helped the weak ones eat and treated the sick ones as best she could. But she felt useless, so big and ungainly now, leaving her cousin and his wife to do the rough work, pulling calves in open pastures, catching the little critters to put on the dehorning paste, finding the lost calves and the dead ones, grafting the orphans onto cows that had lost their own. It went on and on. And Meggie cooked and doctored, went in for supplies and watched the kids and wished her baby had been born months ago so she could get out and do her share in this season when the Double-K needed her the most.

Zach came by on horseback the last Saturday in March, which was the day before Easter. Meggie's heart seemed to expand in her chest at the sight of him. Maybe he would have news of Nate.

But he only said he'd been checking the cows in a pasture that bordered the Double-K and decided to stop in and see how she was getting along. His eyes widened when he looked at the size of her stomach, but he was too well mannered to say anything about how big she'd grown.

Meggie had a pot of minestrone soup warming on the back burner of the stove. She served him a bowl.

Since they'd been friends for so long, she felt comfortable ribbing him a little about Tess DeMarley. "I hear the two of you have been seen around town."

"Tess is a good woman," he said quietly.

"And a pretty one."

"Yes, that's so."

"And I hear she knows ranch life. And loves it."

"You heard right."

"Some other man will snap her up, Zach. Don't drag your heels."

He pretended to glare at her. "Meggie, don't crowd a man."

She laughed and let the subject drop. Zach had been hurt pretty bad once when it came to love. It made sense he wouldn't be rushed the second time around.

"Good soup," he said, and then smiled wryly. "Maybe you ought to sell this place. You can come on over and cook for me."

"Not a chance."

"Just hoping out loud."

Zach's never-ending quest to find someone to replace Edna Heller was getting to be something of a joke to everyone who knew him. Meggie asked, "So who's cooking over at the Rising Sun now?"

"Her name's Angie Iberlin. She's a widow, in her fifties. Her biscuits could sink a battleship, but she's not half-bad at keeping the place clean. And she's polite. That's a real plus in someone who answers your phone, believe me."

"So you're saying that she's working out?"

"I'm saying I haven't done better since Edna left. Just cross your fingers this one will last."

She almost teased him a little more about Tess. After all, if he married Tess, he'd have his housekeeping problem solved. Everyone said that Tess DeMarley was a model of womanly accomplishment. But Meggie thought she'd probably teased Zach enough for the time being. So she kept her peace. Instead of Tess DeMarley, they spoke of the eight bred heifers that had been rustled off the Rising Sun just a month before. Zach said they still hadn't a clue as to who had committed the theft. Meggie wished she could reassure her friend that the theives would be caught in the end. But it didn't look likely at that point, and she and Zach both knew it.

"You doing all right over here?" he asked just before he got up to go.

"I've got Farrah and Sonny. We're managing."

"Maybe you ought to take on an extra hand, just for the next few weeks, until calving season's past."

"I've put the word out, but so far, nobody's knocking down my door."

"I'll check around for you."

She thanked him and then walked him back out to his horse. As she watched him prepare to mount, her heart set up a clamor in her chest. Each beat seemed to echo a name: *Nate, Nate, Nate, Nate,* tempting her, *taunting* her to ask after the husband she hadn't seen in months. If she was going to ask, it must be now, before Zach rode away.

"Zach?"

"Yeah?"

"Do you...hear anything from Nate?"

He paused with one foot in the saddle, then hoisted himself up. "Not a word," he said, once he'd found his seat.

She looked down at the worn boards of the porch.

"I'm real sorry, Meggie."

She looked up and gave her friend a smile. "Hey. It's not your fault. You take care, now."

He saluted her and turned his horse for the gate.

Meggie stayed on the porch to watch him go, thinking that lately no one seemed to know much about Nate. Even Dolores hardly mentioned him anymore—other than to say he was gone most of the time.

Meggie had begun to feel as if he were fading from the world she knew. As if someday soon, Dolores would write and say he'd given up his apartment.

He would disappear completely, find an entirely different life for himself. And Meggie would never see— or hear—of him again.

Nate's private line was ringing when he let himself in the apartment after flying home from a five-day surveillance gig in Boca Raton. He had a cracked rib and a black eye, both caused by a run-in with the object of his surveillance—a hotheaded type who hadn't appreciated having his picture taken. Nate had managed to escape with the information he needed, but he'd lost a very expensive camera. Also, his side hurt like the devil and his head felt as if some fiend was in there with a hammer and an ice pick, pounding away.

He got the door open and bolted to the phone, catching it just before the answering machine switched on. "Yeah, hello?"

"Happy Easter—a day early." It was Zach.

Nate pressed his sore side, wincing, silently calling himself a damn fool for not letting the answering machine do its job. Lately, he found himself driven to break speed records whenever the phone rang. He never intended to get near Meggie again. But a phone call might bring news of her, news that something had gone wrong, that there was a problem with the baby, that Meggie needed him....

"You there, Nate?"

"Yeah. What's up?"

Zach didn't hedge. "I stopped by your wife's place today."

Nate blinked, dropped into the green chair and then groaned as his cracked rib protested. "So?"

"It's calving time around here."

Nate pressed his side some more. "Get to the point."

"Meggie's big, Nate. Really big with that baby you gave her. Before you dumped her."

Nate closed his eyes and said nothing. He was used to being the bad guy. His cousin's hard words didn't bother him much. But having to listen to him say Meggie's name did.

Zach went on, "I know you, Nate. I know there's more going on here than I understand. More than you or Meggie will ever explain to me. But an eight-months-pregnant woman running a ranch at calving time without enough hands to do the work—it's not good."

"She didn't hire anybody?"

"Is that a question?"

"Yeah."

"She says she put the word out, but got no takers. I did a little calling around, and I can't come up with anyone, either. I suppose I can send one of my own men over. It's not like I have them to spare. But for Meggie—"

"All right."

"Pardon me?"

"You heard what I said."

"Good. Cash says he'll fly the Cessna down to Denver to meet you. So let us know when you're coming in."

No way, Nate thought. Cash would bring Abby and Abby was just too damn much like the sister he'd never had. Nate would get lectured on what a low-down rat he'd been to Meggie all the way from Denver to Sheridan. "I'll manage on my own. Thanks."

"Nate—"

"I said, I'll manage on my own."

"I'll tell Meggie you're—"

"Tell Meggie nothing. I'll get there when I get there. Understand?"

Zach sighed. "Sure. As long as you're coming, and soon."

"I'll get the next flight out. Is that good enough?"

"I guess it'll have to be."

Sunday, though they couldn't afford to do it, Sonny, Farrah and Meggie took a half day off. They hid eggs in the yard for the kids to find. And they drove into town to go to church. Then they went back to work.

On Monday, Sonny and Farrah rode out early, as usual. Meggie saw Katie off to the school bus and then took Davey around with her as she did her chores. The day passed uneventfully. Katie came home at three and took Davey back to the bunkhouse with her.

About three-thirty, Sonny and Farrah appeared, leading a prolapsed cow.

"We decided to let you handle this," Sonny said, his eyes gleaming with humor.

"Thanks." Meggie didn't bother to inject any gratitude into the word.

Farrah went on in to check on the kids. Sonny took the cow into the shed off the main corral and coaxed her into the chute. When he had her in, he winked at Meggie. "She's all yours."

Meggie considered using a plastic sleeve, but that gleam in Sonny's eyes made her sure he would razz her that she didn't need a sleeve for a little job like this. Just looking at that smirk of his got her rancher's pride up—as he knew it would.

Meggie stripped off her down jacket and the sweater she wore underneath it. Then she rolled up the sleeve of her maternity smock and moved behind the cow.

The prolapsed umbilical cord was swelled as round as a cantaloupe, and flame red. Meggie tried to lift it gently, to see if the cow could get a little relief, since she probably hadn't emptied her bladder in a while.

But nothing happened. Very carefully, Meggie began the delicate process of trying to ease the prolapse back where it had come from. It was important to be gentle, to take it very slowly.

After what seemed like a lifetime, Meggie finally managed to accomplish the goal. The umbilical cord slid back inside the cow where it belonged.

By then, the cow had voided both her bladder and her bowels. Repeatedly. Meggie had a good amount of the stuff—and quite a bit of blood, as well—splashed on her jeans and shirt. Also, her hand had gone right into the cow with the retracting prolapse.

The cow seemed a lot happier, though. She took cake from the trough in front of her and crunched away on it as if she'd never had a care in the world. Meggie waited, to be sure the cow was really settled down before she pulled out.

Right then, out in the dirt drive that turned around between the bunkhouse and her own house, Meggie heard the sound of a vehicle barreling in, tires spraying gravel as it braked. Sonny's hound barked out a warning.

Meggie felt the cow tighten up a little at the noise. "Go see who that is," she commanded. "And make that dog quiet down."

Sonny marched off to do her bidding. A moment later, she heard him order the dog to be silent. The barking stopped. A vehicle door opened and closed.

Meggie held still, listening to the cow munch on the cake, waiting for the interior muscles to relax a little more.

"Meggie..." Her cousin's voice came from behind her, full of something Meggie didn't like—wariness or worry, she wasn't sure which.

She turned her head. Between the wide-open doors of the shed, right beside Sonny, stood Nate.

Chapter Twelve

Meggie could only gape. She must be seeing things.

But no, he was real. His black hair gleamed in the thin spring sunlight. He had a livid black eye and a frown on his full lips.

He took in Meggie's situation at a glance, and moved swiftly to the other end of the cow. Quietly, he spoke to her, petting her forehead, saying soft, tender things.

Meggie felt the muscles inside the cow relax. Slowly, she eased out and stepped back. What was splattered on her pregnancy-paneled jeans and smock was also thick and pungent all the way up her arm.

Sonny, his face all pinched up in disapproval of Nate, handed her some medication. She poked it inside where her hand had been. She asked, "Any string around here?" Sonny came up with some packaging string. Meggie used it to stitch up the cow, and then, as a final preventive measure, she administered a shot of penicillin.

"You can have her back now," she said to her cousin.

"Terrific," Sonny replied, with a minimum of enthusiasm.

Meggie, her foolish heart racing in joy, turned to Nate. Masking her elation at the sight of him, she gave him a long, assessing stare. "What happened to your eye?"

"A minor disagreement with an object of surveillance."

"You favor your right side."

He shrugged. "A cracked rib, I think. It'll heal."

She went on looking at him. He looked right back. His eyes gave nothing away—beyond a kind of grim determination.

Whatever he'd come for, it wasn't a reunion. She would bet her favorite cutting horse on that. Her silly heart settled into a more reasonable rhythm.

"I want to clean up," she said. "And then we can talk."

Meggie took a long shower. Then she put on a clean pair of pants and a tunic-length sweater, dried her hair and went downstairs.

Nate was waiting at the kitchen table. As she walked toward him, she tried not to shuffle. She couldn't help feeling like the cow she'd just treated, and hating the way he watched her, so distant and measuring.

She pulled out the chair opposite him and sat down as gracefully as she could—which wasn't very graceful at all.

"When's the baby due?" he asked.

"The first of May."

"A month."

"Yes."

A silence descended and hung as heavy as a lead weight between the two of them. She knew he was counting. "So that means you were—what? About four months pregnant before I figured it out?"

She refused to shrink from the accusation in his eyes. "Just about."

"You knew you were pregnant. And you didn't tell me."

"Yep. I wanted to stay with you. Pretty stupid, huh?"

He gave no answer, only went on looking at her with that remote, brooding stare.

The baby kicked. Meggie put her hand on her belly and rubbed, looking down at the spot, letting a small, soothing noise escape her.

When she glanced up, he was still watching her. At that moment, she dared to think she saw tenderness in his eyes, but not for long. He announced flatly, "I'm staying, until the baby comes."

Her foolish heart leaped. But her mind knew better. "Why?"

"To help out."

Meggie rested a hand on the table and studied her short, ragged fingernails.

"I'm staying, Meggie," he said, as if her silence implied argument.

And it did. She didn't want him around if he was going to brood and sulk and watch her with eyes as hard as a banker's heart. "It's not necessary for you to stay. We're doing all right."

"Who's working the herd with Sonny?"

"Farrah."

He grunted, a very self-vindicated sound.

"Farrah's doing just fine," she said defensively. "She works hard, and Sonny takes up the slack. And I...do what I can."

A cold smile played at the corners of his mouth. "I saw. You looked damned uncomfortable standing there with your hand inside that cow and your belly out to here."

"I did fine by that cow."

"Whatever. You need help around here. There's no shame in admitting what you need."

She met his eyes square on. "I'm fine, Nate. Go back to L.A."

"No. That's my baby you've got inside you. Maybe I'll never be much of a father to it. But I can ride a horse and pull a calf—things you can't do right now. You're going to have to let me take care of this damn ranch of yours so you can ease up and take care of yourself for a while."

"I *am* taking care of myself."

"Fine. And now you'll take *better* care of yourself."

The baby kicked again, right in the spot where Meggie's hand already rested. She rubbed it some more.

"Meggie. You know I'm right."

She did, of course. It *was* his baby, too. And if he wanted to take some of the burden off her now, she owed it to him and their child to let him.

With some effort, she pushed herself to her feet. Her back ached, and she rubbed it, sighing a little, making no pretense now that her burden didn't tire her. "Bring your things in. You can take the front bedroom upstairs."

He looked up at her. "Are you really all right?"

She saw the concern in his eyes, all mixed up with

the coldness and the determination to remain indifferent to her. She forced a smile. "Doc Pruitt says there's nothing wrong with me that a few more weeks and several hours of labor won't cure."

"The baby's healthy?"

"As far as anyone can tell."

"What about your cousin?"

"What about him?"

"I could tell by the look he gave me that I'm not his favorite person."

"I told him the truth."

"What truth?"

"That you helped me out to keep the Double-K, and now you want your freedom back—as we agreed from the first."

"Hell, Meggie," he said grimly.

"I just got sick of all the lies, Nate. And I couldn't see any reason to keep telling them anymore, anyway."

He let out a long, weary breath. "Fine. The question is, will he work with me?"

"I'm sure he will."

"I'm glad *you're* sure."

"We'll talk to him tonight."

"Terrific," he muttered as he rose. "I'll get my bag."

Sonny and his family and Meggie and Nate all ate together that night in Meggie's kitchen. It was an ordeal of hard looks between Sonny and Nate, worried glances between the women—and acting up from Davey, who had the radar of most children and seemed to sense that things weren't right with the grown-ups.

Meggie hardly ate a bite, which worried Farrah all

the more. "Are you all right?" she asked. "Are you sick?"

"What are you talking about?" Nate demanded. "She told me today that she's fine."

"She *was* fine." Farrah shot him a glare. "Until *recently,* anyway."

"Are you going to throw up, Aunt Meggie?" Kate asked, her eyes wide. "I could get you a bowl if you are. Mommy always gets me a bowl."

"No, Katie," Meggie said gently. "I am not going to throw up. I am not sick. I just don't have a big appetite tonight, that's all."

"Yucky, yucky. Hate cawots," chanted Davey. He picked up a handful of boiled carrots and dropped them over the edge of his high chair onto the floor.

"That's enough, young man," Sonny said sternly.

Davey beat on his chair tray and chanted, "No, no, no, no...."

"That does it," Farrah murmured. She stood, scooped Davey into her arms and started for the door. He wailed and cried and flailed his fists, but his mother just kept going. His outraged wails continued as she carried him down the short hall, through the living room, out the front door and across the yard to her own house.

The rest of them ate in silence for a while.

Finally, Kate said, "Daddy, I'm all done. Mommy bought some Tootsie Pops. Can I go home and have one?"

"You go right on, baby."

Kate rose, as well behaved as her brother was wild, and carried her plate to the sink, where she rinsed it and stacked it on the counter, ready to wash. Then she went to Meggie's side. "I think I'll kiss you good-night now, Meggie."

"Good night, honey." Meggie put an arm around Kate and kissed her on the cheek, a favor that Kate then returned.

"Should I kiss you, too, Daddy? Just in case I go to bed and you're not home yet."

"Good idea."

More kisses were exchanged.

Then Kate looked at Nate, a frown creasing her smooth brow. "Who hit you in the eye?"

"Katie..." Sonny warned.

Nate actually grinned. "It's all right. An angry man hit me."

"Did you hit him back?"

"Well..."

"That's enough, Katie," Sonny said. "Go on back to the house."

Kate started to leave, then turned back to Nate. "Good night," she said sweetly.

Nate nodded. "Good night, Katie."

Once Kate left, the three adults ate in silence for a few minutes—minutes that seemed to Meggie to crawl by like centuries. Then Sonny rose to carry his plate to the sink.

Meggie knew that in a minute he would be leaving for his own house. She cleared her throat. "Sonny?"

He set his plate down and turned. "Yeah?"

Meggie shot a glance at Nate. No help there. His face was impassive, his eyes fathomless.

She forged on. "Sonny, I suppose you're wondering what Nate's doing here."

Sonny tipped his head to the side. "Well, yeah. I suppose I am."

"Nate's come back to help out for a while, until calving time's through."

Sonny leaned on the drainboard, his wary expression turning to one of frank disapproval. "You mean he'll be leaving you again, right?"

Meggie dragged in a breath and answered carefully, "Sonny, he hasn't come back here for me. He's come for the baby's sake, to help out, since we're shorthanded right now."

Sonny looked down at his boots. "Well. That's real big of him."

Meggie glanced at Nate again. His face betrayed nothing beyond a watchful, bleak patience. "Sonny," she said. "You're wrong to blame Nate for...what's happened. I told you before that he only did what I begged him to do. He helped out a...friend. And he got nothing for it. In fact, it's cost him. To be here through summer and fall, he lost—"

"Stop it, Meggie," Nate said.

She shook her head. "No, I want to say this. I don't think Sonny understands that you missed months of work to be here when I needed—"

Meggie stopped in midsentence as Nate stood. "There's no point in going into this." He winced and pressed his hand against his injured rib. He turned to Sonny. "Look. I'm here to help out for reasons that should be pretty damn obvious to everyone. You're going to have to work with me. Can you handle that?"

Sonny looked at Nate for a long, hard time. Then he shrugged. "I can do what I have to do, sure."

"All right, then," Nate said.

Sonny echoed, "All right." He looked at Meggie. "Thanks for the fine dinner. I'll be going home now."

Meggie murmured good-night and Sonny went out

the same way Farrah had, through the house to the front door.

"Don't make excuses for me," Nate said into the silence Sonny left behind. "I don't need them or want them."

"I was only trying to make him see—"

"People see what they want to see."

"But Sonny is a reasonable man. I think if he really understood all you've done for me, he would—"

"Drop it."

Meggie mentally counted to ten. "Fine." She pushed herself to her feet and went about the task of cleaning up after the meal.

"Where's the dish towel?" Nate asked belligerently a few moments later.

She snared the towel from the towel rack and tossed it to him. He set to work drying the pots and pans while she finished wiping up the counters. When the pots were all put away and the counters gleamed, Meggie went into the living room to watch a little television before she turned in.

Nate went straight upstairs to the front bedroom without even bothering to say good-night.

Chapter Thirteen

In the days that followed, Nate discovered that Sonny Kane was a man of his word. He'd agreed to work with Nate, and he put his personal disapproval aside to do what had to be done. Before long, Nate even started to wonder if Sonny and his wife had decided that maybe he wasn't so bad after all.

It was Meggie who drove Nate crazy. Even with her huge belly leading the way everywhere she went, she drew him just as she always had. And the attraction went far deeper than physical desire. She seemed so peaceful within herself, so content with the burden she carried around. He'd always admired her. And now he admired her more than ever. He not only wanted her—he wanted some of that peace she had.

Sometimes, when he looked at Meggie now, a question would come sneaking into his mind. He would wonder why the hell he was doing this: to her and to himself. Why did he continue to refuse her? Why did he continue to push her away?

He would look at her and think, *She is my wife.* And there seemed to be such rightness, such completeness, in that thought.

He would remember all the years he had stayed away from her. And he would see his future, remote from her and their child. And his solitary life would start to look more like a sentence than a choice; the emptiness inside him would seem all at once aching and vast.

But then, at night, when sleep finally found him, he would dream old dreams, of a dark place. Of the smell of musty wool. Of a vow he had made to himself long, long ago.

Someday I will be free....

He'd wake in the morning certain once again that all he wanted was to get through calving time and be on his way.

At first, Meggie hesitantly attempted to bridge the gap between them. At breakfast, she would ask him things like how he'd slept and did he need anything from town. He answered her questions curtly—"I slept fine and I don't need a damn thing from town"—trying not to be drawn in by her. There were, after all, a thousand and one ways she could get to him—from a bright smile to a gentle word, to a tender look across a room. He tried to keep his heart armed against her.

And she caught on quickly, as she always had. Within forty-eight hours of his arrival, she began beating him at his own game, looking away before he did. Asking no questions that didn't absolutely require answers. Staying clear of him whenever possible. Marking time. Until calving time passed. And he would be gone.

And, though he knew it was unfair, he resented her

for giving him just what he'd been asking for. He wanted to grab her and shake her. He wanted to break through that wall she'd put up around herself as armor against his own indifference.

He wanted her to reach for him. So that, at least for a little while, he could allow himself to be touched.

But she didn't reach for him.

The tension between them seemed to grow by the hour. Sometimes, he felt as if he might explode. Yet, through a pure effort of will, he reined in his temper most of the time—except when she took stupid chances with her health. Then, he felt justified in letting his temper get loose.

After all, he'd come to help out so that she could take it easy. But she refused to take it easy. She would not stop working. Even though Farrah stayed home more now and offered to take on Meggie's work with the animals, Meggie wouldn't hear of that. She insisted on treating the sick and weak stock herself.

She would spend hours with a calf that wouldn't suck. About a week after Nate's return, Sonny brought in a spindly black Angus calf that must have been premature; it simply refused to eat. The mother cow came with it, her bags swollen with unsucked milk; she wore that bewildered look a cow gets when something's not right with her calf.

Since the cow was tractable, Meggie started out each feeding session trying to coax the calf to feed from the source. She'd get herself into a backbreaking, half-bent-over stance, her own belly an obstacle to be both protected and worked around. Holding the calf's head steady, pressing her own cheek up against the side of the cow, she'd stick the fingers of one hand in the calf's mouth while she tried to pump milk into it with the other hand.

Finally, when her arms were running with milk to the elbow, she'd give up on the direct approach. She'd milk the cow into a bucket, stick a rubber teat in the calf's mouth and force milk into it that way. Through the whole procedure she'd whisper soothing, gentle things. And then four or five hours later, she'd do it all again.

One night, when she came in from the shed with milk drying on her arms and down the front of her shirt, Nate told her he wanted her to let Farrah do the feeding from now on. "Or let me," he added, "if Farrah's got something else to do."

"I don't mind."

"You should mind. It's too much for you right now."

"I know what's too much for me. I can handle feeding a few calves."

"I mean it, Meggie. You're through feeding calves. As of tonight."

She gave him one of those looks of hers. A look no woman that big eyed and pretty ought to be able to manage. "I know what I can handle, Nate. Don't you try to tell me I don't."

He reminded her about Abby, who had insisted on finishing a semester at the University of Colorado last year when she'd been pregnant with Tyler Ross. Abby had pushed herself to the brink, and ended up with something called eclampsia that had put her in a coma and almost caused her death.

"Eclampsia is extremely rare, Nate, and there's no proof that it's caused by stress," Meggie told him.

"Oh, so you're an expert on the subject, huh?"

"I know what it is. And I'm not going to get it."

"You're pushing yourself."

"I am not. And I'm through discussing this."

"The hell you are."

"Please don't swear at me."

He started shouting then. "Dammit, you have to take care of yourself!"

She remained maddeningly calm. "I am taking care of myself."

"You're taking chances...but not anymore."

"What do you mean by that?"

"I mean, *no more feeding calves.*"

She looked him up and down, a slow, dismissing kind of look. "Don't try to make my decisions for me. You won't succeed." Then she turned around and headed for the stairs.

"Meggie, get back here!"

She didn't stop; she didn't even glance back. She just left him there in the kitchen, wanting to chase after her, wanting to shout at her some more, wanting to do a lot of things to her that he didn't dare even think about.

That happened about a week after he came back. And every day after that, he found something she needed to be lectured about.

One morning in the barn, when he'd brought in a half-frozen calf for her to warm up with one of the propane heaters, he warned her that she'd better stop driving the pickup.

"I know you drove Katie out to the bus stop today," he accused, as she was making the calf comfortable on a bed of straw.

"It was freezing. And it's a half mile out to the stop."

"If Katie needs driving, Farrah will have to do it."

"Farrah went out with you and Sonny at the crack of dawn."

"Meggie. Hear me. *Do not drive the pickup*. If you need to go somewhere, I'll drive you. Or Farrah or Sonny will. Understand?"

Meggie rose, with some effort, from her kneeling position in the straw. Panting, she glared at him. "Fine. Whatever you say." Then she turned around and lumbered out the barn door.

Nate shrugged. She could stomp off all she wanted. She wouldn't drive that pickup again if she knew what was good for her.

He looked down at the calf, a little black-baldy. It was a miracle, really, how fast heat could work on them. When he'd found the little critter, he'd looked half dead. And yet now, already, he was lurching around trying to get up.

Farrah came in and stood by Nate. "How's the little feller doing?"

"Take a look. Meggie went to get some milk for him—I think."

"You *think*?"

"She's mad because I told her not to drive herself around anymore."

Farrah made a noise in her throat. "Don't see why she's mad. Doc Pruitt already warned her about driving, now she's so big."

"He did?"

Farrah met Nate's eyes and then shook her head. "Now, why do I want to go and get myself between the two of you? Forget I said that."

But he didn't forget.

That night, Farrah made dinner for everybody. During the meal, Meggie asked Farrah to drive her to her appointment with Doc Pruitt. "It's tomorrow. At ten-thirty. Do you think you can take me?"

"I'll take you," Nate said. He wanted to have a few words with Pruitt, find out if there was anything else Meggie shouldn't be doing that she hadn't bothered to mention to him.

Meggie blinked. Clearly, she'd only intended to rub it in to him that she wouldn't be driving herself. The last thing she'd expected was for Nate to volunteer to do the job. She knew how he tried to avoid being alone with her, even in a vehicle. "Farrah can take me."

"I said, I'll take you."

"Farrah—"

Farrah exchanged a quick, grim glance with Sonny. "Leave me out of it. Please."

The next day, Nate made sure to be there waiting, with the GMC running and all warmed up, when Meggie came out to leave for town. She gave him a sour look through the driver's side window, but she didn't say a word, just waddled on over and lugged her weight up into the passenger seat.

They rode the whole way to town in silence.

At the clinic, Meggie signed herself in. The receptionist gave her a little cup and asked her for a urine sample.

When Meggie returned from the bathroom and took a seat in the waiting room, she didn't even glance his way. She buried her nose in a tattered magazine with a picture of Cher on the cover. Nate looked around for something he could read. But women's magazines and kids' books were all he could find.

After about a century, Trudy Peltier stuck her head out the inner door. Trudy was Pruitt's assistant, and an old classmate of both Meggie's and Nate's. "Meggie, come on in," Trudy said.

Meggie put down her magazine and got to her feet.

Nate rose and followed right along behind her. When she realized he planned to go in with her, Meggie turned around and gave him another of her sullen looks. But she had sense enough not to try to tell him to keep out.

"Well, Nate Bravo," Trudy said in that too-sweet way of hers, "isn't it nice to see you here with Meggie for a change?"

"Think so, huh?" He gave her a long, cold look.

She pursed up her lips. "Now, now. No need to get snippy."

Nate just went on looking at her. The black eye he'd brought back from Boca Raton had faded almost to nothing by then. But still, he was sure Trudy could see it and that she was making judgments about him because of it. She had never been a big fan of his. She flashed him a wide, fake smile and then asked Meggie to step on the scale. "My, my," she clucked. "You're gaining nicely."

"Too nicely," Meggie murmured when Trudy finally stopped nudging the counterweight down the bar.

"This way." Trudy led them to an examining room. "The doctor will be with you in a few minutes."

When Trudy closed the door and left them in the small space, Meggie wiggled up onto the examining table and Nate took the visitor's chair in the corner. They sat and waited, both trying, as they usually did lately, not to make extended eye contact.

But the room was too small. Nate had to look somewhere. Once he had studied the color poster of the human heart and read the nutrition chart with its cartoon renderings of happy fruits and vegetables, his gaze just naturally turned Meggie's way.

She had more fortitude; she steadfastly refused to look at him. She sat awkwardly on the end of the examining table, her hands resting in what was left of her lap, her gaze cast down.

Nate studied her bent head, and couldn't help noting the way her shoulders drooped and the sad curve of her mouth. She looked tired and a little dejected. He often saw her rub at the base of her spine, as if it troubled her. He wondered if it ached now.

He stood. "You want this chair? Until Pruitt comes?"

She looked up and blinked. His tone had been gentle, for once. It must have surprised her. "Oh. No. I'm fine." She put her hand at her back and sat up straighter for a minute, stretching her spine a little.

"Sure?"

"Positive."

He stood there for a moment, then dropped into the chair again, feeling like a fool. She took to watching her knees once more. And he looked at her. He studied the soft curve of her cheek and wondered at the thickness of her dark hair, remembering in spite of himself just what the silky strands felt like when he ran his hands through them or pressed them against his mouth.

Finally, Pruitt came in. He greeted Meggie, then nodded at Nate. "Good to see you."

"Same to you, Doc."

Over the years, Nate had been in to see Doc Pruitt more than once—for everything from a persistent case of strep throat to a bone or two he'd broken riding bulls in the local rodeos.

Nate watched the doctor take Meggie's blood pressure and perform a thorough examination. As he tapped and poked and prodded, the old guy murmured things like, "Um, yes. I see. Fine."

When Pruitt stepped back and told Meggie she could button up, Nate saw his chance. "Doc?"

"Hm, yes?"

"Are there any...special precautions Meggie should be taking right now, for the baby's sake?"

Doc Pruitt frowned. "Did she stop driving her pickup on those rutted roads out at the Double-K?"

Meggie shot Nate an indignant glance and jumped to her own defense. "I did. I stopped."

"Well, then, I'd have to say that what we have here is a very healthy, very pregnant woman who appears to be taking dandy care of herself. Just take it easy, Meggie and—"

Nate leaned forward in his chair. "That's it, Doc. That's my point. She won't take it easy. She's got to hand-feed every damned orphaned calf herself."

Meggie glowered at him. "That's not true. I'm careful. I do take care of myself. And the baby."

"Tell her, Doc. Tell her she's got to ease up."

Doc Pruitt looked at Nate, then at Meggie, then back at Nate again. "Hmm. I think the last thing I want to do right now is to get in the middle of a private discussion between a man and his wife."

Nate snorted. "What the hell are you saying? This is a medical question. A question of Meggie's health. And the baby's, too."

The doc patted Meggie's hand. "It's real sweet that he's so concerned. Tell him to get more rest and to eat right. He'll need his strength for when the baby comes."

Meggie grinned. "Right, Doc."

Nate wanted to throttle them both. "I fail to see the damn humor here."

"You take care of yourself, Nate," Doc Pruitt said.

"And, Meggie, from here on in, you come see me once a week."

"I'll make an appointment before I go."

"Hmm, yes. Sounds good."

"Hey, wait..." Nate began, but the doctor had already opened the door and stepped out into the hall.

Before she went home, Meggie wanted to buy groceries. Nate went into the market with her and then wheeled the cart out to the parking lot and loaded the shopping bags into the big lockbox in the back of the pickup for her, so she wouldn't strain herself.

"Oh, and I want to stop off at Cotes's," she said just before they headed for home. "I ordered a few things for the baby and I want to see if they came in yet."

Cotes's Clothing and Gifts took up half of a huge old brick building on Main. Nate dropped her off in front of the store and then told her he'd keep the motor running for her, since all the spaces along the street were taken. But then, just after she disappeared inside, a Bronco pulled out of a space right in front of the store. Nate turned the GMC into the empty spot.

A few minutes passed. Nate began drumming his hands on the steering wheel, wishing to hell she'd hurry up.

Then he started wondering if Barnaby Cotes could be in there with her. Since his father had died a few years before, Cotes had take over the store. And he'd always been after Meggie. Nate could just see the little weasel now, leaning across the counter at Meggie, smiling that slimy smile of his, stalling on telling her the status of her order just so he could keep her there a few more minutes and drool over her. It wouldn't mean a damn thing to Cotes that Meggie was married and eight months pregnant. Nate had seen the way Cotes looked at Meggie. The smarmy little twit would take Meggie May any damn way he could get her.

Nate had just begun to contemplate the idea of marching in there and dragging Meggie out, when she emerged on her own. She had a shopping bag in her hand and a sweet, happy smile on her face.

He knew for sure then: Cotes had been buttering her up.

She spotted the GMC and shuffled over to it, then pulled open the passenger door and dragged herself up into the seat. She shut the door and turned her smile on him—not on purpose, just because he happened to be sitting there. "Thanks for waiting for me."

He glared at her. Her smile faded to nothing. He shoved the old pickup into reverse, making it lurch when he let off the clutch. Beside him, Meggie buckled her seat belt and looked straight ahead.

She didn't speak the whole way home—and neither did he. When they got to the house, he carried her groceries in without saying a word, then changed into work clothes, tacked up the bay mare he'd been using and set out to join Sonny in the South Pasture.

For the next week, Nate avoided even minimal conversation with Meggie. He knew if he ever said more than a few words to her, he would say too much—about Cotes, as well as about the way she refused to take care of herself. Avoidance seemed to work pretty well. They shared a few testy exchanges, but somehow he managed to keep from losing it so bad they had a full-blown fight.

Then on Wednesday, the sixteenth, a spring blizzard blew in. It came in fast, rolling down from the Big Horns, turning the world blind white in a matter of hours. All Nate, Sonny and Farrah could do was find their way back to the buildings and wait inside for it to blow over.

For the whole of that afternoon, they were stuck in the houses. Since Meggie had been handling most of the cooking lately, they gathered at her house until after dinner, playing checkers and double-deck pinochle, while the wind screamed outside and, beyond the windows, it looked like midnight in the middle of the day.

The power went off around four, but it wasn't a big problem. Sonny fought his way around the side of the house through the driving snow and got the generator going. Both houses and the outbuildings had electricity again by four-thirty. And there was plenty of wood in the lean-tos built against Meggie's house and the bunkhouse. They could last indefinitely, cozy and warm inside, no matter how brutal the weather outside.

But the calves were another story. A calf didn't take the cold well. It's short coat would quickly soak through. Unless it could huddle against its mother or find a sheltered spot out of the wind, a calf out on the range could freeze to death quickly in a bad spring storm.

And Meggie was worried about how many of them this storm would take from her. She tried not to show it, since she was a practical woman and didn't go around moaning when moaning would do no good anyway. But Nate felt her worry as if it were his own. He watched her, the way she would glance toward the windows when she thought no one was looking, as if she might at last see something beyond them but a wall of whirling white.

She could usually wipe up the table with her opponents at pinochle—which was why Nate liked to partner up with her. But that day, she forgot which cards had been played and she got caught reneging twice.

By the time evening rolled around and Sonny and his family had struggled across the yard to their own house, Nate was starting to think that he would go nuts watching her try to pretend she wasn't half-crazed with anxiety. He found the whiskey bottle she kept in the pantry and poured himself a couple of fingers, just to settle his nerves a little.

But then, when he went out to the living room and sat down to enjoy his drink, she was standing at the window, looking out at the darkness, and at the snow driving against the panes. His nerves started singing all over again, just looking at her.

"You won't make it stop by staring at it," he said, maybe a little too harshly.

She turned, saw his drink and frowned.

He dropped to the sofa and took himself a warming sip. Then he shrugged. "What?"

She sighed. "I just don't think you should start drinking now, that's all."

"It's one drink, Meggie. That's all it is. One drink is not *starting drinking*."

She pressed her lips together and sighed again. "Fine. Whatever." She turned and headed for the stairs.

He raised his glass to her. "Right. Run off."

She stopped, smoothed her hand down her belly. She looked so frustrated and sweet and ripe he wanted to strangle her—or kiss her. Or both. "Let's not get into it, Nate."

He leaned forward and set his glass on the coffee table in front of him. "Get into what?" he asked, as if he didn't know.

She shook her head. "There's no point in talking to you." She took another step toward the stairs.

"Wait."

She glared at him—but she did stop. "I mean it, Nate. I don't want to fight with you."

He rose. She looked so vulnerable, even with that angry frown on her face. He wanted to touch her. He wanted to—

Her eyes widened. "Nate, don't."

He'd moved to within a few feet of her. And out of nowhere, he heard himself asking the question that had been eating at him for days. "Last Friday, in town. Was Cotes there when you went in his store?"

She shook her head and sighed. "Oh, Nate..."

"Was he there? Just tell me."

She studied him for a moment, then admitted, "Yes."

"I knew it."

"Why are you looking at me that way? There's nothing between Barnaby and me."

"Tell that to Barnaby."

"This is ridiculous."

"The hell it is. He'll be after you, you know that, once I'm out of the picture. He's going to think he's got a chance with you, that you're going to need a husband to help you raise our kid."

"Nate, stop it."

"I'm just telling you."

"Fine. I heard you. Now, let's drop it."

"Will you say yes to him?"

She made a low, incredulous sound in her throat. "I can't believe you're asking that. You have no right in the world to ask that."

She was right; he knew it. He'd let himself get completely out of hand here. The storm, her fear for the calves, all the damn tension caused by having to be near her and not being able to touch her, was finally pushing him over the edge.

He made himself lift his shoulders in a lazy shrug. "Consider the question retracted."

She studied him for a long, bleak moment. Then she nodded. "Can I go to bed now?"

"Go."

She turned and left him there, with his half-empty drink and the howling, lonely sound of the wind.

By the next morning, the storm had blown on by. They woke to a white and silent world. The power had come on again, so Nate went out and turned off the generator. Then Meggie served him breakfast.

Nate, Sonny and Farrah rode out with the sun, which shone harshly on the new snow, blinding them with its reflected glare. They found calves weak, sick and dying in the pastures, stretched out and stiff the way they got when the cold took them.

Right away, they got three warming huts set up—sheds with propane heaters in them—in the pastures farthest from the home place. All day they loaded calves into the GMC and Meggie's pickup and carried them to where they could get them warm.

In the barn and the corral shed closest to the house, they had heaters going steadily. Meggie worked as hard as the others, tending the calves they brought in to her.

By the end of the day, they were all about to drop from exhaustion. But the situation with the calves didn't look as bad as they had thought at first. Most of the them were at least a week or two old, ready and able to suck again as soon as they got warmed up. In general, it turned out that if a calf was still breathing when they got to it, it survived. After they warmed it up, it could be turned right back to its mother—given that its mother could be found, which wasn't always the case.

Orphaned calves meant more hand feeding, at least until they found a cow that would take on the motherless one. And though the season had started to wind down, there were still a few day- and two-day-old calves. Even after they'd been next to a propane heater for a while, some of them wouldn't suck.

Which meant that at nine-thirty that night, Meggie was still out in the shed. She had her fingers down the throat of a big newborn Charolais-cross, trying to get him to take a little nourishment.

Nate worked right beside her, feeding another of the calves, one that seemed to be doing pretty well. Once the calf Nate was tending had finished eating, he took a minute to make it comfortable in the straw under one of the heat lamps.

Then he went to stand above Meggie. "It's time to turn in."

She looked up at him, her eyes flat with exhaustion. "You go on."

"Meggie—"

"I won't be but a few minutes. Really."

He didn't believe her. She'd stay out here all damn night, more than likely. But he was too tired himself to argue with her.

"Come in soon. Or I'll come out and get you."

"I told you. A few minutes, that's all."

He decided to take her word for it and left her there, with that half-dead calf. It seemed as if it took every ounce of energy he had left to drag himself into the house and trudge upstairs, where he stripped and stood under the shower for a while.

When he came out, all he wanted to do was fall across a bed and not get up for a year or two.

But he knew that woman too well. He hadn't heard her come in. Because she *hadn't* come in.

Muttering crude things to himself, he pulled on his boots and yanked on his jacket and went out across the frozen yard to drag her bodily back to the house, where she belonged.

He found her sitting in the straw, the calf's limp head on her knees.

She looked up at him. "He died," she said. "He just gave a big, tired breath and that was it. His eyes rolled back." She looked down at the sprawled body, then put her hand against the neck, as if some flutter of pulse might still beat there. "Such a waste." She shook her head, stroking the smooth hide. "A waste of a fine animal."

Nate understood. It wasn't the death so much. A rancher lived with death, day in, day out. In the end, a rancher fought for the lives of his animals—in order to take those lives.

But Meggie had a good touch and a powerful will. She had put her mind and heart and hands into saving this animal. For nothing.

He dropped to his haunches beside her in the straw. "You're beat. It seems worse than it is, you're so tired."

She just went on slowly stroking the calf's neck.

"Meggie."

Still, she kept up that stroking, dried milk gleaming like snail tracks along her arm. Raising her other hand, she waved absently at the air. "Leave me alone. I'm okay. I'll be in soon."

"Meggie…"

"I mean it. Go."

"No. You're coming in."

Her hand stopped its stroking for a fraction of a second. And then she shrugged. The stroking began again, a total dismissal of him and his demand.

His anger, always right beneath the surface lately, rose up. His blood felt hot in his veins. He controlled the heat, channeling it into determination.

Damn her, she would do his will in this.

Slowly, deliberately, he reached out and put his hand on the back of her neck, below where she'd anchored her hair out of the way.

She stiffened. He held on.

The smoothness and warmth of her skin stunned him. The little hairs at her nape felt like the softest strands of purest silk.

God. How long had he kept himself from touching her?

Too damn long.

She batted at his hand. "Don't."

He kept his hand right where it was. His blood pounded in his veins, a primitive, possessive rhythm. "Come inside. Now."

She looked up at him then, her eyes widening, the flat, defeated exhaustion turning to something else. Something that burned him even as it surrendered to him.

"Nate…"

"Now."

"I don't want—"

"Now."

He felt her shudder—and then give in completely, the stiffness leaving her as she relaxed under his hand. Carefully, tenderly, she eased the calf's head from her knees and onto the bed of straw beneath them. The cow she'd milked to do the feeding shifted nervously nearby. She gave it a look. "Easy," she whispered. "It's okay, now."

"Meggie." He rubbed his thumb on her nape.

She turned her big eyes on him. "What?"

"At some point, you've got to let it go."

"I know."

He gave a tug, to pull her close. She sighed and drooped against him, her head fitting into his shoulder, her arm finding its way around his waist.

"So tired," she murmured.

He stroked her hair. "It's all right. All right...." He kissed her forehead. "Come on, now. Let's go in."

He helped her to stand. Once on her feet, she leaned heavily on him and glanced blankly around her at the heat lamps suspended from the roof of the shed, at the three other calves still recovering from the effects of the blizzard the night before—all orphans, as far as they knew now.

"Everything's fine," Nate told her.

She looked down at the sprawled, lifeless body of the Charolais calf. "We should—"

"I'll see that it's taken care of. In the morning."

"I just wish—"

"Shh. Let's go."

She acquiesced to be led by him, out into the icy spring night, across the yard and into her house.

Chapter Fourteen

Inside, he helped her out of her jacket and hung it by the door, shrugging out of his own and hooking it there, too. He sat her down and took her dirty boots from her. Then he led her up to the room they had shared in the summer.

In the bathroom there, he removed the rest of her clothes, peeling them off swiftly, letting them fall to the tiles at her feet. Her eyes had gone blank on him again. She looked down at her big belly and her swollen breasts and then up at him, as if she wondered how she'd gotten there, in the bathroom with him, naked.

He turned to the tub and worked the faucets, getting the water running and hot, then pulling the lever that would engage the shower nozzle. He tested the temperature and stepped back. "Get in."

She turned obediently to do as he'd told her.

"Wait."

She stopped. He pulled her close to him and worked at the big tortoiseshell clip that held up her hair. The clip opened. The heavy, red-shot brown waves dropped to her shoulders. He couldn't stop himself. He buried his face in the strands. They smelled of hay and milk, of dust and sweat. Of Meggie in her most elemental form.

She made a small, questioning sound. He raised his head from the silky mass and smoothed it on her shoulders. "Go on. Get in. Wash your hair, too. Wash everything. You'll feel better once you do."

She got in under the shower spray, pulling the curtain closed behind her. He leaned against the wall, watching her blurred shape through the semiopaque curtain. She took a long time. The room filled up with fragrant steam, warm and wet and soothing. He was there, holding her towel, when she pushed back the curtain and stepped, dripping wet, from the tub.

He handed her the towel. As she dried herself, he got her heavy winter robe from the back of the door and held it up for her. She handed him the towel and slipped her arms into the sleeves of the robe. He moved behind her and began drying her hair.

"Hungry?" he asked.

She shook her head. "Just tired."

He dropped the towel atop the pile of discarded clothes. "Come on."

But she resisted.

"What?" he asked.

"My hair's too wet. If I go to bed with it this way..." Her voice trailed off, as if she'd forgotten in midsentence what she'd set out to say.

"All right." He got her blow-dryer from the little cabinet under the sink, feeling a strange kind of elation that he knew where it was, that he had been a true husband, at least for a while. One who knew the things a husband knows: where she kept her hair brush and her aspirin, her blow-dryer and the lipstick she so seldom wore.

He plugged in the dryer and handed it to her.

A few minutes later, he took it from her and put it away. Then he led her into the bedroom, where he switched on the lamp beside the bed.

He pulled back the covers, smoothing them down. Once all was in readiness, he turned to her, untied the robe and took it away from her.

Totally unconcerned about her own ungainly, pregnant nakedness—and so incredibly beautiful to him— she took a pillow from the pile at the head of the bed. He watched as she climbed in and curled up on her side, tucking the pillow under the heavy bulge of her stomach—for support, he realized.

"Comfortable?" he asked.

She made a low noise in the affirmative.

He settled the covers around her. And that was it. The moment when he should leave her.

But he couldn't leave her.

He backed up and dropped into the small armchair a few feet away. By the light of the lamp between them, he looked at her soft face. Her eyes seemed bruised, she was so tired. And her clean hair shone against the white pillowcase.

Those bruised eyes held a deep sadness. "I don't want to go on like this," she whispered. "It hurts, Nate. And it makes me so tired."

He knew exactly what she meant. It hurt him, too. This forced closeness they lived in, the armed camp each inhabited in the same house, the hostility that grew between them, filling the echoing, lonely space left by the intimacy they had once shared.

"I just want…to lie down with you." The low words came out of him all by themselves. "Let me, Meggie. Let me do that. Tonight." Some tiny part of him that still had scruples felt shame to ask such a thing of her.

But not enough shame to keep him from asking.

She sighed.

"Meggie."

She closed her eyes—and then opened them again.

He chose to take that as consent and rose quickly. He yanked off his clothes and his boots, tossing the clothes across the chair, shoving the boots against the wall. She watched him, her eyes sorrowful and knowing and full of hopeless yearning.

When he lifted the layers of blankets to slide in beside her, he half expected her to tell him no. But she said nothing, only scooted back enough to give him room.

And then at last, he was there with her, where he'd dreamed of being for months now, wrapped up warm and close, the fresh-showered scent of her taking all his senses. With a groan, he pulled her against him. She came—sighing, soft, willing, sad.

She kissed him, a long, slow, hungry kiss. Her belly pressed against him, and her heavy, ripe breasts, too. She reached down and touched him, a loving touch that turned to stroking.

"No, Meggie…" he groaned.

"Shh…"

He lost it, like some kid who'd never known the feel of a woman's hand.

Shattered, shamed, he threw an arm across his eyes and looked away from her.

She only pushed back the covers and went to the bathroom for a towel.

A little later, she lay beside him again, in the warm cove the blankets made. He reached for her. And he began to touch her. He could no more stop himself from touching her right then than he could make himself quit breathing. He had to feel every inch of her, to know her again as he had known her before, when they were man and wife, when he had allowed himself to forget for a while that freedom was what he wanted most.

This time, instead of facing him, she lay tucked right into him, spoon-fashion. That gave him free reign to caress her, and also put his body in the best, most complete contact with hers.

He found her somehow softer to the touch than before. Her skin felt hotter, too. And if most of her seemed softer, that didn't include her belly. The hard tautness of it astounded him. He rubbed the stretched skin gently, felt a movement. She sighed and put her hand over his.

"Does it hurt when he kicks?"

"Not too much. Not most of the time."

His hand strayed up to cup her full breast. And then down again. All the way down.

"Is it all right?"

"Yes. Carefully. Oh, Nate. Yes."

He touched her, his fingers parting her, delving in. She moved against him, eager, hungry, totally his. Within moments, she cried out.

As her ragged breathing slowed, he pulled her even closer than before, his body absorbing the heat of hers.

"Sleep now," he whispered.

"Oh, Nate…"

"Just sleep."

* * *

In the morning, before dawn, Meggie woke and slid out from under the blankets. Not allowing herself to glance back at the warm bed and the man sleeping there, she pulled on her robe. Then she tiptoed around the room, taking clean clothes from the bureau and closet, pulling them on quickly, staying as quiet as she could.

Downstairs, she built up the fire, put on the coffee and whipped up batter for pancakes. Nate came down just as she was pouring the first batch on the griddle and cracking eggs into a pan.

"Sit down," she said.

He came and stood by the table, looking sheepish and vulnerable. "Meggie, I..."

"Sit down," she said again.

He dropped to the chair. She moved around the room, pouring him coffee, turning the pancakes, then sliding them onto a warm plate along with three eggs. She set the food in front of him. "Eat."

He spread butter, poured on syrup, then picked up his fork.

A few minutes later, she joined him. They ate in silence, until the food was gone.

Meggie pushed her plate aside and sat back in her chair.

Nate looked at her broodingly from his end of the table. "All right. What? I shouldn't have last night. I know."

"I love you," she said.

He turned away, toward the still-dark windows that looked out on the yard behind the house.

She folded her hands on the table, stared down at them, then up at him. "Last night was...beautiful for me."

He looked down, up, toward the window again. Everywhere but at her.

"Nate? Did you hear me?"

"I heard." He spoke harshly—and then added in a ragged whisper, "And it was...the same for me."

She waited for him to look at her. But he didn't. So she asked, "Where are we going together, Nate?"

He shrugged, still looking toward the dark windows.

"Are you my husband?"

He said nothing.

"Nate. I think you're going to have to decide."

He made himself look at her then. "I just...I came to help out."

She closed her eyes, breathed deeply, and leveled her gaze on him again. "For calving time."

"Right."

"Calving time is almost done."

"Not quite done."

"Enough so that we can manage now without you."

His expression darkened. "What are you talking about? We drove ourselves to the brink yesterday. You need me. If I hadn't been here—"

"It was the last big storm. You know it. And most of the cows have calved." She thought for a moment. "But come to think of it..."

"What?"

"You're right."

He looked at her sideways. "About what?"

"About how I need you."

He made a scoffing sound. "I meant you need my help, here, now, to run this damn ranch of yours."

"And you're right. I do need your help. I always will."

"What are you getting at?"

"Well, branding time comes next. And then the spring drive. And after that, it'll be summer, which means haying, mending fences, trying to keep the weeds down. It goes on and on. You know it does. So you're right, I do need you. The Double-K needs you. Your baby needs you. And not just for now. Forever."

She watched his defensiveness turn angry. He didn't like words like "forever." "You won't get any forever from me, Meggie. You knew it all along."

"Yes. I did."

His lip curled in a snarl. "But still you came after me."

"Because I love you. I told you from the first—if I needed a child to keep my home, I wanted that child to be yours."

He made a low, derisive sound. "Hell, Meggie. What is it with you?"

"What do you mean?"

"You know what I mean. You live in some crazy romance inside your own head. You have...no damn judgment at all."

She opened her mouth to speak, but he ran right over her.

"After all," he sneered, "you went and chose me as the object of your undying love. That's pretty damn deluded, if you think about it—first that you chose *me*. A losing proposition if there ever was one. But even if it had been someone else, someone not quite so... impossible as I am, it's still nothing more than some big, pointless fantasy, telling yourself for all these years that there's only one man in the world for you. It's not normal. No one carries a torch for that long."

Meggie refused to be shamed by his cruel words. She

faced him proudly. "Maybe you're right. Nobody does. Nobody in the world—except me."

"Oh, so you're something rare, are you?" Her rose, his chair scraping the floorboards as he stood. "Something special, in your delusion?"

"Stop it." She pushed herself to her feet so she could meet him eye-to-eye, grunting a little with the weight of the baby. "Just stop that mean talk. It won't work on me anymore. I'm not some poor nineteen-year-old girl now, someone you can reduce to tears with a few cruel words. I've lived with you, and I know you in the deepest ways. And sometimes, in the best of our days together, I've dared to dream that it would work out all right between us."

He just looked at her, so hard and guarded. "Stop dreaming. It'll get you nowhere."

She gave his own hardness right back to him. "Fine. Then it's time for you to go. For good and all. It's time I stopped dreaming of what will never be. And it's time you stopped hanging around here, angry all the time because you want me, but then not letting yourself have me. If you want to see someone who's deluded, you just take a good, long look at yourself."

That reached him, for some reason. His hard mask of angry defensiveness slipped. He allowed her to see the pain underneath. "Meggie, I…"

"What?" She looked straight at him.

He gazed back at her hopelessly.

"Say it," she prodded. "I can take it. I've taken so much. You've got no idea how strong I am."

"I just…can't be what you want me to be."

She shook her head. "That's not true."

"Hell, Meggie…"

"No. Listen." She leaned toward him across the table, as much as she could with her stomach in the way. "You *are* what I want you to be. I've never asked you to change."

"You want me to come here." He gestured with a sweep of his arm. "To live here. To spend my life working the Double-K. With you."

"That's so."

He grunted, a vindicated sound.

She added, "But it's not the only option, not as far as I'm concerned."

He frowned and dropped his arm to his side. "What are you saying?"

"I'm saying that I learned something in November when I lived with you in L.A. I learned that…I could make my home anywhere. If there was love enough. If there was you. I'm saying that I would go with you. Me and our baby. If you would take us. Wherever you wanted to go."

He gaped at her. "You really mean that. You'd leave the Double-K."

"I would. For you. To be with you." She smiled at him then, a sad, resigned smile. "But you won't take us, will you?"

"I…"

"Will you?"

Slowly, he sank back to his chair.

With a sigh, she sat down, too, and waited for him to answer her. He said nothing. And that was all the answer she required.

She rested a hand on the swell of her belly. "Oh, Nate. I swore to myself, on the morning after our wedding night, that I would take the time we had together and find joy in it—and not ask for more. I've tried to do that. I truly have. Maybe I didn't always succeed.

Maybe I…hoped more than I had a right to. Maybe I held on longer than I should have. But when you finally said it was truly over, I accepted your will. I came home and set my mind to leaving you behind.

"But then, you wouldn't stay away. You had to come back, temporarily, for calving time. And maybe you're right. Maybe we wouldn't have made it through without you. But it's no good, the way you treat me now. It's as if you have to hurt me. You've been riding me all the time, picking fights with me over every little thing. And then, finally, when neither of us could bear it anymore—you fell into bed with me. For what? To relieve the tension a little? So you can start the meanness all over again?"

"Meggie, I didn't—"

"Don't lie to me. Lie to yourself if you have to, but not to me. You want me, but you won't stay with me. You can't keep your hands off me, but you won't be my husband. I'm not going to take it anymore. It isn't any good for me, or for our baby."

Outside, the sky was beginning to lighten. Meggie pushed herself upright again and picked up her plate, as well as his. She carried both plates to the sink and set them down carefully.

Then she turned to Nate once more. "You're going to have to make up your mind, Nate. For good and all. Do you stay and make a real marriage with me—or do you go?"

He looked toward the window and the coming dawn. Out in the yard, one of Farrah's roosters crowed. Sonny's hound took up the cry, letting out one long, doggy wail to the new day.

"Nate. Make up your mind."

He turned to her then. She knew his answer before he spoke. She could see it there, in the loneliness of his eyes.

"All right," he said at last. "I'll go."

Chapter Fifteen

Not long after breakfast, Nate rode out with Sonny. But before he left, he kept his word about the Charolais calf. Meggie never knew where he took it, but when she went out to the shed to feed the other calves, it was gone.

Nate stayed for two more days, until all the calves weakened by the blizzard were back on their feet again. Through that time, he and Meggie were unfailingly kind to each other. Kind, and as polite as strangers.

On Sunday, after breakfast, Nate rose from the table and went back upstairs.

Ten minutes later, he came down. Meggie was in the living room, feeding wood into the heat stove. She shoved in a log and shut the small iron door in the side of the stove.

"Meggie."

She rose and faced him. He carried that big duffel he used as a suitcase.

She rubbed her hands down the sides of the jumper she wore. Inside her, the yearning rose up, to reach out, to whisper, *Don't go....* She pushed the yearning back down, into the deepest part of her, where it made a dull, never-ending ache.

"Well," she said in the false, bright voice she'd been using with him for the past two days now. "You're all ready."

"Yeah." His tone was gruff. "All packed and ready."

"All right, then."

He seemed to struggle with what to say next. "If you need me..." he began.

She shook her head. "I'll let you know. When the baby comes."

"Thanks."

"And I'll send the papers, as soon as I get out of the hospital."

"Papers?"

"For the divorce."

His jaw tightened, and then relaxed. "Good enough."

They stared at each other.

He shrugged. "Well. Goodbye, then."

"Goodbye, Nate. And...thank you."

He actually grinned. "What for? Making you miserable for weeks on end?"

"You know what for. If there's ever anything I can—"

He put up his free hand. "Don't."

She closed her eyes, bit her lip and nodded.

"Goodbye, Meggie."

She nodded again, because her throat had tightened up and she didn't think she could push any words through it. And she kept her eyes closed, so she wouldn't have to watch him go. She heard his boots moving toward the door.

And then they stopped. "Meggie?"

She made herself open her eyes.

"The other night, when I asked you about Cotes...that was wrong of me. You said it then—I had no right to ask a thing like that."

She still didn't speak. She couldn't.

"Meggie, what I'm trying to say is, if you find someone you think you could make a life with—even if it's that smug little twit Cotes—I want you to go for it. All right?"

She swallowed and managed to whisper, "All right."

It was a lie, of course. There would be no other men for Megan Bravo. She was like her father. A person who gave her love only once. She felt in her heart that Nate knew she lied.

But he didn't let on. He only gave her one last too-brief smile. And went out the door.

How did she live through that parting? It was worse than it had been when he sent her away after Thanksgiving, as if a big piece of her heart had been torn out.

Yet Meggie was a strong woman. And she had her land and a baby to live for. She knew that as calving time passed and the first wildflowers begin to appear in the snow-patched meadows, she would find peace inside herself once more.

Nate had no such expectations. Peace was a word in a language not his own.

In the days immediately following his departure from the Double-K, he slept little. Every time he did, he dreamed the dream of darkness. Of musty wool. Of his vow to get free.

Or else he dreamed of Meggie. Calling him. He saw her eyes, looking into his, just the way she had looked at him when he went out her door that last time: a look of undying love—and pure determination to get on with her life.

Without him.

He knew that he could not go back to her. Ever. That he had to leave her alone to put her life back together again.

And he *would* leave her alone.

He swore to himself that he would.

Maybe he would move. His neighbors all seemed poisoned against him. They had adored Meggie. And they blamed him for her departure.

Rightly so.

For five years, he'd lived just fine with their indifference. But their simmering resentment set his teeth on edge. That damn Dolores looked at him as if he'd just done murder and buried the evidence.

On Tuesday, two days after he returned to L.A., Nate took a job tracking down a runaway, a kid of fifteen who'd stolen his father's Mercedes and gone south. Nate found the kid on Wednesday night, in a seedy bar just over the Mexican border.

It was a disaster. The kid had taken up with some teenaged gangster types. The gangsters had guns. Nate ended up in a shoot-out, and took a bullet in the left arm, midway between the shoulder and the elbow. The gangsters got nervous. They ran out, guns blazing, and jumped into the Mercedes. They took off, peeling rubber—and leaving the runaway in tears in a back room.

The barmaid, a kindhearted type, poured tequila over the bullet hole in Nate's arm and then wrapped it in a bar towel. The kid, by that time, was more than willing to go home.

They started back around three on Thursday morning. The trip was pure hell. Nate's arm burned as though someone had stuck a hot poker in it, and the kid cried the whole way, swearing that his parents didn't care about him, that all he wanted was his freedom.

Near Blythe, just before dawn, Nate pulled over to the side of the road. "Get out."

The kid sniffed and gaped. "Huh?"

"You want your damn freedom, you got it. Get out."

The kid blinked, then looked frantically out the windows. The highway was deserted in both directions. A lone Joshua tree stood a few feet from the passenger door. "It's the middle of the desert. I can't get out here."

Nate scowled across the distance between them. "You want your freedom or not?"

The kid whimpered. "I just want them to care about me."

Nate carefully pressed his arm and wished with all his heart for some heavy-duty painkillers.

"Don't kick me out, mister."

Nate let out a growl. "Then don't tell me one more damn time about how you want freedom. I've had it up to here with freedom. Understand?"

The kid gulped and nodded. "Yeah. Okay. I got it. Sure."

"You hungry?"

"You bet."

They stopped at a McDonald's for Egg McMuffins and reached the Malibu beach house where the kid lived at a little before noon. The kid's mother made a big fuss over him. The father, however, seemed more concerned about the loss of his Mercedes than anything else.

"Do you have any idea what a machine like that costs?" the man demanded, when he and Nate were alone to settle up.

Nate mumbled something unintelligible—he always tried to be unintelligible when he wanted to say something he knew wouldn't be wise.

"And you'd better have someone look at that arm," the man suggested with distaste.

"I'll do that." Nate found himself thinking *to hell with wisdom,* and added, "You know, if you cared half as much about your kid as you do about your car, he probably wouldn't be risking his life hanging around with gangsters."

The man gaped. "I beg your pardon."

"You heard me."

The man's ears turned red. "I want you out of my house. This instant."

Nate couldn't help grinning. "I guess I'll get no referrals from you, huh?"

"Out."

Nate left, heading over to Cedars, where he had the bullet dug out. Then, at around four in the afternoon, armed with a vial of codeine tablets, he went back to his apartment.

The codeine worked great. At five, after an unsatisfying shower where he tried not to get his arm wet, he fell across his bed and slept for a drugged, blessedly dreamless twelve hours.

He woke at five in the morning. His arm was throbbing again. Somehow, he managed to pull on his jeans, though his arm screamed in pain as he did it. Then, unwilling to go through the agony that putting on a shirt and shoes would have cost him, he dragged himself into the bathroom and washed down another codeine with water straight from the tap.

It occurred to him then that he hadn't eaten since the Egg McMuffin yesterday morning. So he wandered down the hall toward the kitchen, stopping on the way to gather up two days' worth of mail; it had gotten scattered around the floor a little when he came in the evening before. In the kitchen, he flipped on the light. And groaned at the sudden brightness. He switched the light off. It was that time of half-light, just as the sky began to brighten. He could see well enough to make coffee and toast. And the mail could wait a little longer for his attention. He threw the pile of envelopes and circulars on the table and went to brew the coffee and make toast.

When the food was ready, he sat at the table to eat, wishing the codeine would kick in and stop the throbbing in his arm.

He saw the movement in the parking lot out of the corner of his eye. He turned to look, glad he'd left the light off or he never would have noticed.

Two skinny guys were sneaking around down there. One carried what appeared to be a crowbar. And the other had some kind of handgun.

Not good news for whoever they were planning to visit.

Community Watch to the rescue, Nate thought grimly as he picked up the phone and dialed 911. He reported two armed prowlers and gave his address. Then he got his own Beretta 9 mm, shoved in a loaded clip and headed for the door.

Nate crept down the stairs, wishing the Tyrells had left their porch light off, keeping to the side wall, his bare feet making no sound on the smooth concrete steps. At the bottom of the stairs, he waited, listening, pressed against the wall inside the enclosure provided by the stairwell. He heard nothing.

Slowly, he made his way around the side of the building, moving silently, even breathing with care. When he peeked around into the parking lot, he saw no one.

Beyond the lot loomed the carports, each one a dark cavern with the end of a vehicle sticking out of it. Terrific places for bad guys to hide.

Nate waited some more, listening for a giveaway noise, alert for any movement. He saw and heard nothing. He was just trying to decide whether he wanted to chance cutting across the open parking lot to get to the carports, when he heard splintering noises, then a window being shoved up.

The sounds came from somewhere on the other side of the building next door. Nate sprinted across the driveway that ran between the buildings, then raced around the laundry room. He saw a figure disappear through a pried-open window on the ground floor. Nate knew whose window it was: Hector Leverson's. On the other side would be Hector's living room. Since Nate saw no one else, he assumed the other prowler had gone inside first.

A number of choices presented themselves, none of them particularly appealing. He could wait for a response to his 911 call. Maybe they'd show up in time to handle the situation.

He could try Meggie's technique and set up a racket. That might possibly make the prowlers—who had just attained the status of burglars—break and run. It also might freak them out enough that they'd shoot Leverson, if the poor guy was home.

Nate's third option was to crawl in the window after them. They had thoughtfully left it open for him, after all.

Nate just couldn't resist that open window. He approached it with caution and crouched below it for a full sixty seconds, listening for sounds from inside, thinking that the good thing about a little excitement like this was that it got his adrenaline up and he could hardly feel his throbbing arm at all now. But then, of course, that could just be the codeine starting to work.

A light went on, in a window several feet down the wall—in what he judged would be Hector's bedroom. He heard a cry, slightly muffled, a cry that seemed to come from the room where the light had just come on.

More than likely both scumbags had stalked their prey there. Which meant the living room would be deserted—he hoped.

Muttering a short prayer to the patron saint of fools and PIs, Nate slid over the sill and into the dark living room. His bare feet hit the floor soundlessly and he stayed crouched low when he landed, weapon ready.

Luck was with him. There was no one there. But from the bedroom, he could hear voices speaking in low, intense tones.

He rose to his feet and moved silently across the floor, to the short hall that branched two ways—straight on toward the front door and to the left toward the bedroom and bath. He turned left and then plastered himself against the wall, moving as close as he could to the open bedroom door.

He listened.

"Please—" that was Leverson's voice "—there's money there. On the bureau. Take it and go."

"You got more stashed around here somewhere," one of the scumbags insisted. "I know you do. I got a sense about this stuff. You've got yourself a hidey-hole. I would have found it last time if we hadn't been...interrupted."

"No," Leverson said. "I keep my money in the bank. I swear to you. What's there on the bureau is all we have on hand."

We, Nate thought. Leverson wasn't alone? That would make four people in that room.

He listened, to place them.

He heard footsteps. And rustling sounds. "There's only about fifty bucks here." It was the same scumbag who had spoken a moment before.

"That's all you'll find in this apartment." Leverson's voice again.

"You come up with more." Bingo, Nate thought. Scumbag number two. "Or the woman gets it."

"I will, I will. I'll...go to my bank, withdraw all I have," Leverson said. "Just, please. Don't hurt her."

"Don't beg them, Hector." Nate's heart stopped. He knew that voice. "They're low-life trash. You don't beg low-life trash."

The second scumbag muttered something foul. Nate heard the thudding impact of what might have been a fist or a pistol grip against flesh. Then he heard his mother's groan.

"Now," said the first man. "The bitch is quiet. And we want more money, or—"

"Or what?" Nate stepped into the doorway and aimed his Beretta at the man who'd spoken last.

For a moment, everyone froze. Nate found himself noting the fact that his mother and Hector Leverson were wearing matching pajamas.

Then the first scumbag swore. And the second scumbag turned the .38 special in his hand away from Sharilyn toward Nate.

"No!" Sharilyn cried.

Nate opened his mouth to warn her not to move. But he was too late. She launched herself across the bed and threw herself in front of him.

The scumbag fired his .38.

And pandemonium broke out.

When it was over, Nate had the guy with the crowbar in a chokehold and Hector had beaten the one with the .38 unconsciousness, using a bronze statuette he'd grabbed off of the bureau.

Sharilyn lay on the floor, as still as death, with a .38 slug in her back.

As it turned out, it was a busy morning for the LAPD and prowler calls had gotten low priority. They had to call 911 again to get a patrol car and an ambulance.

Help came right away, however, for a call that included breaking and entering and possible murder. All the tenants came out to see what was happening. Dolores wailed on her husband's shoulder, outraged at all the evil in the world.

Within an hour of the incident, the patrolmen had taken the bad guys away and Sharilyn had been wheeled into an operating room at Cedars for emergency surgery.

Nate stayed with Hector.

They sat in a waiting room and drank bad coffee.

And Hector talked. "The one with the gun," he said for about the tenth time. "That was the same guy who attacked me last November. It's amazing. He actually came back to try again."

"It was his last try," Nate promised, as he'd done more than once already. "Don't worry about him, Hector. They'll lock him up for good now."

Hector lowered his head. "Do you think she'll be all right?"

Nate had to swallow hard before he could speak. "Yeah. Sure. She'll be fine."

"We were married yesterday," he said to Nate, as he'd said already to the tenants and the patrolmen. "It was the happiest day of my life."

Nate was still having trouble dealing with that news. He knew his mother. She had wanted only to be free. And yet, she'd chosen to marry again.

Hector sighed. "She's a wonderful woman. I'm the luckiest man alive."

"Right."

Hector's hands were clenched. "I don't believe in violence."

"Gotcha."

"But I can't help it. I wish I had killed the one who shot her."

Nate grunted. "You did him serious damage, I promise you. His head will never be quite the same."

"Good," Hector whispered. He looked hard at Nate. "She would like to make peace with you, more than anything in the world."

Nate closed his eyes and looked away.

But Hector wouldn't take a hint. "I know, I know. She told me. About the money she took from your grandfather, about how she sent you away. But she really did believe things would be better for you at the Rising Sun than they would have been with her. She never could control you, and she felt that you were headed for trouble. She thought that your grandfather would take you in hand."

"Look—"

"And about the other, when you were a small child. She always felt you were deeply...damaged by that. She feels she should have known earlier. I told her that she has to forgive herself, that she had been so busy trying to support the family all on her own. And at least when she did find out she took action. And it never happened again, did it?"

Nate said nothing. He felt strange. Nauseated, suddenly. And a little light-headed. He thought of the dreams. The dreams of the darkness...

"Are you all right?" Hector was asking.

"Yeah. I'm fine."

Hector's kind eyes widened as understanding dawned. "You don't remember, do you?"

Nate only looked at him.

Hector swallowed. "Oh, God."

Nate's palms were sweating. "What...are you talking about?" As he said the words, he wanted only to call them back.

Hector drew in a long breath and faced Nate. "It's not my place. I was wrong to say anything. I'm sorry. Please. I'm so worried. About her. I'm just not thinking straight."

Nate stared at Hector; he was still talking. But his voice seemed far away. And his face blurred before Nate's eyes, became his father's face, scowling at him, scaring him...

"A man needs some damn freedom in his life," Bad Clint muttered as he pushed Nate into the closet.

Then he closed the door.

And Nate was alone, in the darkness, with the smell of musty wool from the coats and rubber from the rain boots stored back against the wall.

The darkness was all around him, pressing on him, making it hard for him to breathe.

But then, just when he though he would start screaming, he looked down.

And saw the thin line of light that came in beneath the door. As long as there was that thin line, he told himself, he could stand it.

Nate heard the lock turn. And then he got down on the floor where the light was, put his thumb in his mouth. And waited.

He didn't know where his father went. He didn't know what his father did. But he did know that his father would let him out before his mother got home.

"Nate. Oh, please..."

He heard Hector's voice from far away. He waved a hand at the voice absently. He was wondering...

Had there been a time when he protested, when he cried and screamed and fought what his father did to him? He didn't know. Right now, all his memory would show him was acquiescence. And a terrible patience.

A promise to himself that he would wait. To get out. That he would grow up, be a man, eventually. And then, like his father, he would have his freedom. No one would box him in ever, ever, again.

"Please..."

He felt Hector's hand on his arm. He shook it off.

He must have been about five before his mother discovered what his father did with him when she went to work. That was after she somehow scraped enough together to buy the bar and they were living over it. She came up in the middle of her shift one time. And Bad Clint was gone. She called for Nate.

But he stayed quiet, waiting, the way his father always warned him to do.

"If you know what's good for you, you'll keep your yap shut," Bad Clint always said.

Nate heard his mother moving through the apartment, looking in the closets and calling his name.

At last, she opened the door. The light came in, all over him. Banishing the darkness. Making everything all right.

"Oh baby, my baby," she cried as she scooped him close to her body. She was warm and smelled of cigarettes from the smoky bar downstairs. He cuddled against her and didn't say a word.

"Nate…"

Nate shook his head, blinked. And Hector's insistent voice faded into nothing again.

Later, when Bad Clint showed up, Sharilyn was waiting for him. She screamed at him. She told him she'd have him arrested if he ever tried a trick like that again.

"How long?" she demanded, "How long have you been locking him up in the dark like that?"

"A man needs a little damn freedom," was all his father would say.

"I mean it," she told his father. "I will see you in prison if this *ever* happens again."

How Nate loved her then. Fiercely. Totally, for saving him from the darkness, for telling his father he'd better not ever put him in the darkness again.

Nate swore to himself that he would do anything for her. Anything at all.

He ran free after that, until his father died.

And then his mother sold him to his grandfather.

And he learned that she was just like his father: she would do terrible things, just to be free.

He had hated her then, a thousand times more than he ever hated his father. He had hated her more because she had made him love her before she sent him away as if he was nothing to her.

And then this morning, she had taken a bullet in the back to protect him.

It was just possible he would have to reevaluate his judgment of her.

"Nate. Dear God. Nate…"

Nate blinked. And Hector was looking at him, his gentle eyes full of fear and concern.

"Are you all right, Nate?"

Nate armed sweat from his brow, feeling numb and strange and not all there.

Was that it, then? Was a dark closet the place where the hunger for freedom had been born?

Over the years, he'd managed to forget the horror of the darkness. Only the hunger to be free had remained.

Had that hunger served him in any way?

The answer came instantly: yes. It had given him the patience, the will to stay sane, a child locked in a dark place for what must have seemed like forever.

But did it serve him now?

Was it worth the price now—of love? Of connection? Of knowing his child? Of holding Meggie in his arms every night, for as long as both of them lived?

"Nate. Please. I never meant to—"

Nate made himself smile at Hector. "No. It's all right. It's been…a hell of a morning, that's all."

An hour later, the surgeon came out to talk to them. "She's going to be all right," he said.

Hector and Nate went in to see her. She looked pale and she was still unconscious, with tubes taped to her nose and her mouth, and an IV drip hooked up to the back of one hand. She had a huge, dark bruise on her chin, where one of the scumbags had clipped her. Hector pulled up a chair and took the hand that had no needles stuck in it. Nate stood across the bed from him, waiting.

It was a few hours before she woke up. Nate was there when she opened her eyes.

She looked at his face and she knew instantly. She whispered in a papery voice, "I guess things will be all right now between you and me."

"Yeah," Nate said. "If you want it that way."

"I want it."

"Okay, then." He smiled at her. "But next time, if there are guns involved, keep your mouth shut and don't move."

She didn't even bother to reply to that, only whispered, "I heard Meggie left."

"Yeah."

"And that she's going to have a baby."

"Yeah."

Her brows drew together. "I bet you don't want to miss that. Seeing your baby born. It's going to be soon, from what I've heard."

"Yeah. Real soon."

"Then what are you doing here?"

"Well, my mother's in the hospital."

Sharilyn cast a loving glance at Hector. "Don't you worry about me. I have someone special to care for me. You go on home now, Nathan, to Meggie and your baby, where you belong."

Chapter Sixteen

The last Saturday in April, Meggie woke in the morning to a rippling contraction that moved over her stomach and down into the deepest part of her. Smiling, she put her hands over the place where her baby lay.

Over the past several days, her belly had lost its high roundness. Now her baby lay low inside her, ready to be born.

"Um, yes. All right. Very good," Dr. Pruitt had said when she'd gone to see him on Thursday. "Effacement is progressing nicely. And you're even a couple of centimeters dilated. That baby should be showing up here very soon."

Dr. Pruitt had been right, of course.

Very right. Meggie lay in her bed thinking that before the next day dawned, she would hold her baby in her arms.

She rose from the bed and went down to make the

fire. Farrah called from her house just as Meggie got a good blaze going.

"Come on over. Biscuits and gravy."

"I'll be right there." Meggie damped the fire a bit, grabbed her jacket from its hook by the door and went out across the cold, dark yard to the bunkhouse.

Another contraction took her in the middle of the yard. Meggie stopped, put her hands on her stomach again and looked up at the stars overhead.

Not a cloud in sight. Her baby would be born on a sunny day.

Farrah knew what was happening the moment she saw Meggie's face. "How far apart are they?"

"Ten minutes at least, and they're not very regular. It could be quite a while yet."

"Did you call Doc Pruitt?"

"Not yet."

"By nine, though, all right? If the contractions keep up."

"Sure. By nine."

When Meggie called at nine, the contractions were still several minutes apart. Doc Pruitt told her to call again in two hours.

At eleven, he still advised her to wait awhile before heading to the hospital in Buffalo. Meggie cleaned her house and made sure she had everything she'd need for her short stay in the hospital. She checked the baby's room, opening all the bureau drawers to see the little shirts and hand-knitted sweaters, running her hand over the stack of diapers that waited on the shelf above the changing table.

"It won't be long now," she whispered to the yellow teddy bear propped up in the side of the crib.

Lunchtime came and went. Meggie felt too excited

to eat. But Farrah talked her into sipping a little soup and chewing a few crackers.

Finally, around three in the afternoon, Meggie reported to Doc Pruitt that her contractions were coming about every five minutes. They were longer, and stronger than before, too.

"Get Farrah to bring you on in, then," the doctor said. "I'll meet you there."

Meggie put her suitcase in the back of Farrah's little hatchback 4x4. Then she returned to the house to check one last time that all was in order.

Farrah was waiting with the motor running and her kids in the back seat when Meggie came out of the house again. Smiling, she walked across the sunny yard toward the waiting car. She had just reached the passenger door, when a contraction came on. She leaned on the roof of the car, waiting for it to pass.

Farrah rolled down her window. "Okay?"

Meggie groaned. And then she smiled. "Yeah. They're getting stronger."

"Come on, then." Farrah pushed the door open from inside.

Meggie started to lower herself to the seat.

And right at that moment, an old GMC pickup came barreling into the yard.

"Nate," both Meggie and Farrah said at the same time.

Spraying gravel, Nate spun to a stop a few yards from the hatchback. Sonny's hound started barking.

Meggie called out, "Scrapper! You stop that now!"

The dog gave one last "Whuff," then slunk off the side of the bunkhouse porch.

Nate shoved open his door and slid down from the seat.

Appalled by the tenacity of her own unwavering heart, Meggie hungrily drank in the sight of him. He looked wrung out, rakish—and disreputable as always. He was the handsomest man she'd ever seen.

She asked, "What happened to your arm?"

He shrugged. "It's nothing. A scratch."

"That's no answer."

He gave a cursory glance toward Farrah and the kids and the waiting hatchback. "Where are you headed?"

"To Buffalo."

"What for?"

Instead of telling him, Meggie turned and spoke to Farrah through the side window of the hatchback. "Go ahead and take the kids back inside. I'll give you a call. Soon."

Farrah frowned. "Meggie, it's a ways into Buffalo."

"There's time."

"But—"

"Please. Go on in. I'll talk to Nate. And I'll call you soon enough."

Farrah shot a disapproving look past Meggie's shoulder at the man who waited behind her. "If he gives you any trouble, you send him to me. I'll show him the sharp side of my tongue."

Meggie forced a grin, trying to telegraph a confidence she didn't feel. "Will do."

Farrah wasn't buying. "Look, Meggie…"

Meggie pushed back from the door. "Go on. I'll be fine."

Reluctantly, Farrah drove the car the short distance to her own front door, got out and began removing Davey from his carseat.

Meggie and Nate were left standing alone in the middle of the yard, looking at each other. Neither of them seemed to have a clue what to say.

Meggie was the one who broke the silence. "What do you want?"

His mouth opened, and then he closed it. His brows drew together in a pained frown.

She demanded again, "What do you want, Nate?"

His jaw tightened beneath a couple of days' worth of beard. He coughed, and then he asked quietly, "Will you please invite me in?"

She thought of all the times he had left her, of all the times he had sent her away—of how each of those times, he had broken her heart. She didn't want her heart broken anymore. She'd had all the heartbreak she could take. Behind her, the screen door to the bunkhouse squeaked shut as Farrah took her children inside.

"Please, Meggie..."

"You told me you would leave. For good. I believed you, Nate."

"Please."

With a grim sigh, she turned and led him up the steps and in the front door of her house. In the living room, she gestured at a chair. "Sit. And whatever you have to say, it had better be good."

But he didn't sit. He stood in the middle of the room, looking at her with the most intense and burning expression she'd ever seen on his face in all the years she'd known him.

"What?" she demanded. "*What?*"

And he said, "Meggie, I love you."

Meggie blinked. "What?"

He said it again. "I love you."

She gave a small, bewildered cry.

He added, "And there's more."

She gulped. "There is?"

"Yeah. I have always loved you, since the first minute I saw you, minus your Wranglers, on the back of that big sorrel gelding you used to ride. I know I don't deserve you. I know I've hurt you bad every time I walked away from you. You shouldn't take me back. But if you will take me back, I will never walk away from you again. I swear it."

A contraction took Meggie, right then, as Nate was saying all the words she'd made herself stop dreaming she would ever hear from him. She dropped into an old rocker that had been her granny Kane's and, moaning, she let the pain have its way with her.

Nate covered the distance between them and knelt at her side. He felt for her hand. She gave it and squeezed hard, bearing down the way the pain bore down on her.

At last, it passed off and away. She panted and leaned her head back. "Whew."

Nate let out a groan of his own. "My God. You're in labor."

She rolled her head to look at him. "Yeah."

"Buffalo," he muttered in dawning understanding. "The hospital. That's where you were going."

"Right."

He jumped to his feet. "What's the matter with you? Why didn't you tell me?"

"I'm fine, really. I have plenty of time."

"We're going. Now."

She didn't move. "Soon. I promise. Soon."

He dropped down beside her again. "Look. I really think we should get out of here."

"We will. In a minute. But first, there's so much...to decide."

"Not now. Later. Right now, we should be—"

"Listen. I have a ranch to run. You live in L.A. How are we going to work that out?"

"Meggie—"

"Answer me. How will we work out this problem?"

He stood once more and raked his fingers back through his hair. "I can't think about this now."

She wasn't accepting that as any excuse. "If I can, you can. Now, tell me how we'll handle this, or I'm not getting out of this chair."

"All right. Fine." He paced back and forth in front of her. Then he stopped and shrugged. "I don't see it as a problem. I've got nothing against ranching. I'll move back here."

Meggie gaped. This was so crazy. Her wildest, most impossible fantasy come true. "You will? You're serious? You're not just saying it because—"

He knelt once more. "Hell, no. I'll come back. I know how you feel about this place. I expected, if you'd have me, that I'd move back home and work the Double-K with you."

"You did?"

"Yeah."

"Oh, Nate..." She reached out, put her hand against his stubbled cheek, partly in pure love—and partly to reassure herself that this wasn't some crazy, labor-induced dream. He grabbed her hand, kissed her palm. She smiled at him adoringly. And then she frowned. "But all you ever wanted was to get away from here." She pulled her hand away.

"No."

"Yes. You always said—"

He stood again. It seemed he couldn't stay in one place. "Meggie, look. A lot has happened in the past couple of days. I've figured out a lot of things I never really understood before. I'm going to fill you in on all of it. Soon. While we're driving to the hospital, and after we get there. So let's get on the way. All right?''

''What things?''

''Meggie...''

''Just tell me a little. Come on.''

''My mother got married.''

''To Hector?''

''Right.''

''I knew it.'' Her face lit up. ''Wait a minute. I know. You made up with your mother.''

''More or less.''

''Oh, Nate...''

''I was really off base about her.''

Meggie couldn't help it. She felt wonderfully smug. ''I told you so. She really does love you. But people are people. They make mistakes. And I honestly believe she did the best thing for you when she turned you over to your grandfather. Don't you?''

''I do, Meggie.''

''Good.''

He bent down and took both her hands. ''Can we go to the damn hospital now? Please?''

''In a minute. Let me think what else we have to deal with...I know. I would want to go back to L.A. sometimes, to visit Dolores and our other friends there—and your mother and Hector, too. Could we do that?''

''Whatever you want, Meggie. Anything you want, I swear.'' He still had her hands, so he pulled her from the chair. ''Let's go.'' He pushed her ahead of him, toward the door. ''Do you have a suitcase or something?''

''It's in Farrah's car.''

''Fine.''

She turned and faced him before they went out. "Nate, I'm just so proud of you. I can't believe it. You made up with your mother...."

He groaned and rolled his eyes. "Meggie. Out the door. Now."

"I'm going. But listen—"

"No more. We are leaving now." He reached around her, groping for the door handle.

She kept talking. "I just want to say this. I may get clingy sometimes. Especially in the next several hours. And clingy was something I swore I'd never be with you."

Nate looked down into her flushed, earnest face and understood that he couldn't go another minute without holding her. Instead of pulling the door open, he pulled her close.

Sighing, she cuddled against him. He groaned—in pain, this time.

"Oh!" she said. "Your arm..."

"It's okay. It's fine. Don't pull away." He cradled her tenderly, moved beyond imagining by the feel of her huge belly pressing against him and her soft arms sliding up to encircle his neck.

"I really didn't want to be clingy, Nate," she murmured ruefully into his ear.

"Cling to me, Meggie," he whispered against her silky hair. "Never, ever let me go...."

From the *Medicine Creek Clarion* week of
April 31 through May 7:
HELLO, WORLD...
Born: April 26, to Megan May Kane Bravo and

*Nathan Justice Bravo,
a son, Jason James, 7 lbs. 6 oz. Mother and child
are doing just fine.*

* * * * *

*Those cynical Bravo men are dropping like flies!
Watch as Zach Bravo finally marries his true
love—or is she?—in the last installment of*
CONVENIENTLY YOURS.
PRACTICALLY MARRIED *is available in
May…
only from Silhouette Special Edition.*

Return to the Towers!

In March
New York Times bestselling author

NORA ROBERTS

brings us to the Calhouns' fabulous
Maine coast mansion and reveals the
tragic secrets hidden there for generations.

For all his degrees, Professor Max Quartermain has a
lot to learn about love—and luscious Lilah Calhoun is
just the woman to teach him. Ex-cop Holt Bradford is
as prickly as a thornbush—until Suzanna Calhoun's
special touch makes love blossom in his heart.
And all of them are caught in the race to solve
the generations-old mystery of a priceless
lost necklace...and a timeless love.

Lilah and Suzanna
THE
Calhoun Women

A special 2-in-1 edition containing
FOR THE LOVE OF LILAH and
SUZANNA'S SURRENDER

Available at your favorite retail outlet.

Take 4 bestselling love stories FREE

Plus get a FREE surprise gift!

**ALICIA
SCOTT**

Continues the
twelve-book series—
36 Hours—in March 1998
with Book Nine

PARTNERS IN CRIME

The storm was over, and Detective Jack Stryker finally had a prime suspect in Grand Springs' high-profile murder case. But beautiful Josie Reynolds wasn't about to admit to the crime— nor did Jack want her to. He believed in her innocence, and he teamed up with the alluring suspect to prove it. But was he playing it by the book—or merely blinded by love?

For Jack and Josie and *all* the residents of Grand Springs, Colorado, the storm-induced blackout was just the beginning of 36 Hours that changed *everything!* You won't want to miss a single book.

Available at your favorite retail outlet.

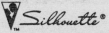